My Life as a Meme

Other Books by Janet Tashjian,
illustrated by Jake Tashjian

The My Life Series:
My Life as a Book
My Life as a Stuntboy
My Life as a Cartoonist
My Life as a Joke
My Life as a Gamer
My Life as a Ninja
My Life as a Youtuber

The Einstein the Class Hamster Series:
Einstein the Class Hamster
Einstein the Class Hamster and the Very Real Game Show
Einstein the Class Hamster Saves the Library

By Janet Tashjian

JANET TASHJIAN

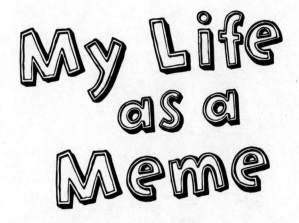

My Life as a Meme

with cartoons by
JAKE TASHJIAN

Christy Ottaviano Books
Henry Holt and Company
New York

Henry Holt and Company, *Publishers since 1866*
175 Fifth Avenue, New York, NY 10010
mackids.com

Henry Holt® is a registered trademark of Macmillan
Publishing Group, LLC
Text copyright © 2019 by Janet Tashjian
Illustrations copyright © 2019 by Jake Tashjian
All rights reserved.

Our books may be purchased in bulk for promotional,
educational, or business use. Please contact your local
bookseller or the Macmillan Corporate and Premium Sales
Department at (800) 221-7945 ext. 5442 or by email at
MacmillanSpecialMarkets@macmillan.com.

Library of Congress Control Number: 2018945027
ISBN 978-1-250-19657-6

First Edition, 2019 / Designed by Patrick Collins

Printed in the United States of America by
LSC Communications, Harrisonburg, Virginia

10 9 8 7 6 5 4 3 2 1

For all the Dereks working hard
to be better readers.

My Life as a Meme

MALIBU!

MATT AND I ARE SKATEBOARDING home from school, when I hit a rock and go flying onto the sidewalk. My knee gets scraped but something more valuable than a body part ends up shattered—the screen on my phone.

scraped

"My mom's going to kill me," I tell Matt. "She just had this fixed from when I broke it last time."

shattered

salvageable

It's only been a couple months since I dropped my phone out the car window trying to snap a photo of a dog in a taco costume. Thankfully, I captured one salvageable picture and was able to turn it into a LOL-worthy meme with a little help from a cool sunglasses filter.

"We need to get helmets for our phones," Matt suggests. "They take more abuse on these boards than our heads do."

I run my finger across the screen. "It looks like it's trapped in a giant spiderweb."

"It's not like you can erase the crack with your finger," Matt says. "I think you're going to have to come clean to your mom."

I tuck the phone back into the pocket of my shorts. I might have to encase my phone in something more protective—maybe bubble wrap or foam. For a minute, I think I've come up with a great invention until I realize my phone would be safe but I'd never be able to actually USE it.

Even with insurance on all the family phones, Mom complains about how much money it costs to maintain them. She doesn't need to say that it's mostly me—and sometimes Dad—because she's still using the same phone she got years ago. My favorite phone accident was when we were at the Thompsons' house and Dad took my phone away because I was running around their pool. But then he didn't look where he was going and fell into the water with BOTH our phones. Dad tried to mitigate the tension in the car

encase

protective

maintain

mitigate

by joking that our smartphones were smarter than we are, but Mom was still furious the whole way home.

After I leave Matt at the top of his street, I try to come up with a good story for yet another broken phone. Maybe some guy knocked me over and tried to steal it? Or it fell out of my pocket while I was rescuing a kid from getting hit by a car? Whatever I end up saying, Mom will probably realize I'm making it up and I'll have to tell the truth anyway. Knowing when I'm being less than honest—in other words, lying—has always been one of Mom's superpowers.

rescuing

When I get home, both my parents are cooking in the kitchen. Mom's wearing scrubs from her veterinary practice next door and Dad's in his workout clothes, which means he just got back from the gym. Mom's latest culinary obsession is using her new pasta machine and she's got Dad halfway across the kitchen holding a long string of dough that she'll cut into noodles on the wooden cutting board. Mom's had a lot of cooking fads over the years but her handmade pasta is one of the better ones. If she grounds me for breaking my phone again, at least an awesome dinner can be my consolation prize.

dough

consolation

The pasta machine is in the same place on the counter where Frank's crate used to be and every time I see it, I think about him. Frank is the capuchin monkey we used to be a foster family for until he had to go

roommate

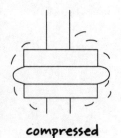

compressed

fettuccini

back to the foundation that trained him. Having a monkey as a roommate was one of the best things ever but we all knew sooner or later he'd have to go back. (Thanks to me and my dreams of YouTube stardom, it was sooner rather than later.)

Don't get me wrong—I love the pasta machine—but it's no monkey.

"Guess what?" Dad folds the compressed pasta carefully onto the counter. "Your mom made an awesome score today."

"I wouldn't necessarily call it a 'score,'" Mom says, slicing the dough into fettuccini. "It's more like I agreed to help someone out and the job comes with some nice perks."

I can see why they call them perks because that's exactly what my ears do as soon as the word leaves her mouth.

"One of my patients has a beautiful home in Malibu," she continues. "Darcy is a tech mogul, on a photo safari at a wildlife reserve in Kenya. She asked if we could dogsit at her place for the long weekend."

dogsit

"She needs a veterinarian to dogsit?" I ask. "Seems a little extreme."

Mom explains that Darcy has several go-to dogsitters, but all of them are taking advantage of the long weekend and going out of town.

"With her favorite vet in charge," Dad continues, "she won't have to worry about a thing. Malibu, here we come!"

My mind ricochets from surfing to hiking to eating clams to swimming. I've never had a bad time when we've gone to Malibu, and this time it'll include a second dog to keep Bodi company. I don't want my broken phone to change that, so I decide to put off telling my parents for a while.

"It's not going to be all fun and games," Mom says. "Poufy isn't like other dogs."

I ask Mom to explain.

"She's the only dog I know with her own Instagram account," Mom answers.

"No way!" I reach into my pocket for my phone but stop as soon as I feel the broken screen. "Wait, this isn't the person who invented that unicorn game app who comes to your office in a limo, is it?"

Mom nods and drops the fresh noodles into the pot of boiling water. "Darcy definitely spoils Poufy, but she's a longtime patient. In exchange for a free vacation in their giant house, we'll be in charge of Poufy."

"How GIANT are we talking?" I ask.

Mom wipes the flour off her hands and scrolls through photos on her phone. "Is this big enough?"

The house in the picture is modern, constructed of floor-to-ceiling glass, surrounded by trees and mountains and with an ocean view. It's five times the size of our house. So what if I have to help take care of a spoiled dog? It'll definitely be worth it to show off pictures of me living it up in paradise.

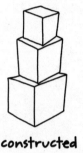

constructed

"We'll each have our own floor!" I say.

Dad smiles. "We were thinking you might want to invite a few friends—there's plenty of room."

I know my parents want me to bring friends so they can spend time alone without worrying that I'll be bored, but I'm still excited by the offer. I immediately text Matt, Carly, and Umberto to see if they're free next weekend.

We're heading to the beach!

Now all I have to do is figure out how I'm going to fix my phone.

WHAT TO BRING

IT TURNS OUT THAT THE BEACH house in Malibu is handicap-accessible, so Umberto will be able to come after he reschedules his Saturday computer class. Carly and Matt also have to shuffle around their schedules, but by the next day at school, they're all locked in.

shuffle

"We should see if Heinz can give us surf lessons again," Carly suggests. Heinz is a surf instructor who

rugged

basically lives in the water giving lessons. His skin is so rugged from spending all his time outdoors, he looks much older than he is.

"You have to find out if the house has any gaming systems," Matt says. "Or if we should bring one of ours."

"It's MALIBU—you're crazy if you don't want to be outside," Carly says. "I think you can go three days without video games."

Umberto, Matt, and I stare Carly down over her turkey sandwich. "I think not," I finally answer.

When Mrs. Cannelini—one of the lunch crew—walks by, Umberto calls her over. "Is it my imagination or did you change the recipe for the mac and cheese?" he asks.

perceptive

Mrs. Cannelini looks at him with pride. "How perceptive! We DID—do you like it?"

While Umberto compliments her on the meal, Matt and I just shake our heads. No one has more pleasurable conversations with grown-ups than Umberto. It's actually a great quality—trying to give people a little boost to their day. Not to mention that Umberto usually gets much bigger portions at lunch than the rest of us.

pleasurable

boost

Carly, of course, has ten different apps on her phone for keeping organized, so she helps us remember some of the things we'll need for our Malibu adventure.

"Not just regular stuff like toothbrushes," she begins.

"Toothbrushes are completely optional," Matt interjects. "People got along fine for thousands of years before they were invented."

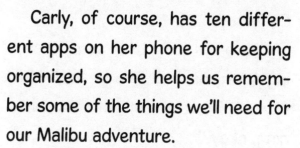

interjects

"Yeah—and they needed dentures before they were twenty."

repellent

moisturizing

getaway

Carly gives him a sarcastic smile that flashes her braces. "We'll need sunscreen, insect repellent, bathing suits, moisturizing lotion—"

"WE DO NOT NEED MOISTURIZING LOTION!" I try to grab Carly's phone but she's too fast and shoves it into her bag.

"It's better to be safe than sorry," Carly says.

"No one's going to be sorry spending three days at the beach," Matt says. "Give it a rest with the planning, okay?"

A Malibu getaway should be ONE thing my friends and I can agree on, right?

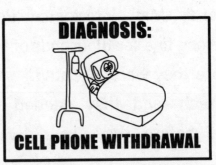

DIAGNOSIS:

CELL PHONE WITHDRAWAL

EXCITEMENT BUILDS

EVEN THOUGH I'M TERRIFIED OF losing gaming privileges on our trip, I finally have to reveal my broken phone to my parents. I don't know if it's because she's looking forward to some beach time, but Mom isn't as angry as usual. She does, however, make me clean out the garage and fold three loads of laundry to reimburse her for the sixty dollars it will cost for a new screen.

reveal

reimburse

When we pick up my phone from the repair shop, Mom makes me promise to buy a stronger case with my birthday money—as if I was trying to wreck my phone on purpose.

facecloth

"If you have to take it with you when you skateboard," she says as she backs out of the parking space, "maybe wrap it in a sock or face-cloth inside your pocket."

"As long as you don't text and skate," Dad adds.

Mom's suggestion might be the silliest thing I've ever heard, but I thank her because I'm happy to have my phone back and want the conversation to end.

As soon as we get home, I head upstairs to see what I've missed online. The repair place only had my phone for a few hours but it feels like decades.

I knew I was going to lose my streak on Snapchat, but seeing the ZERO makes me immediately feel like one too. I open a video link from Matt, which shows a guy bending the tines of a pitchfork with his bare hands. I can't tell if it's real or just edited to look real; either way, it seems not only impossible, but dangerous.

tines

And awesome.

Umberto and Carly both send me the same meme—a sly picture of Captain Jack Sparrow—with text above and below that reads *WHEN YOU FIND A TREASURE CHEST BEHIND A WALL AND IT'S EMPTY.*

sly

It's a funny joke that combines Fortnite with *Pirates of the Caribbean*; I forward the link to Matt.

Caribbean

technology

I've heard my parents and their friends discuss the perils of kids growing up with so much technology at their fingertips but I can't imagine life without my phone, my games, or my tablet. Mom always talks about this incredible information age we're living in, but for me, it's all about the JOKES.

Something can happen with one of your favorite YouTube stars and two seconds later somebody's done a screen grab and turned the funny bit into a meme or GIF for the rest of the world to enjoy. Dad talks about how he used to watch *America's Funniest Home Videos* on Sunday nights—imagine rearranging your schedule around a TV show! Now you can watch puppies jumping into washing machines 24/7—on dozens of different channels—from your phone.

Dad sticks his head into my room and shows me the forecast—a column of bright sunshine and 78 degrees. Bodi must hear me celebrating because he runs into my room wagging his tail.

forecast

"Do you think Heinz can teach Bodi how to surf too?" I ask Dad. "Bodi on a surfboard would be the greatest meme of all time!"

Dad tilts his head to the side. "Your mother didn't tell you?"

I stop smiling. No good news has ever started with those words.

"Tell him what?" Mom walks by my door with an armload of towels.

"Bodi isn't coming?" I pout slightly, hoping to squeeze out enough

sympathy

interact

sympathy to make my parents change their minds.

"Sorry," Mom says. "Poufy's owner doesn't allow her to interact with other dogs."

"That doesn't make sense," I argue. "You're a professional!"

"Yes, and when they make appointments, Darcy pays for an extra hour to make sure no other dogs are with Poufy in the waiting room," Mom says. "Bodi will be fine without us for a few days. I asked Cindy from my office to take care of him while we're gone."

"But Bodi's the best!" I argue. "He was great with Frank. You know he'll behave with Poufy—which, by the way, is the worst name for a dog EVER."

Mom tells me the conversation is

over and goes back to packing. I reach behind Bodi's ears and give him an extra-long scratch.

Dad looks both ways and puts a hand to the side of his mouth like he's about to tell me a secret. "Did we mention this place has a trampoline?"

trampoline

It takes me less time to pack than Carly spent TALKING about packing.

OFF WE GO

collapse

BILL, UMBERTO'S VAN DRIVER, drops him off at our house Saturday morning and shows Dad how to collapse Umberto's wheelchair for the ride. They lift Umberto into the backseat of the SUV, while Mom chats with Carly's mom by the car. I'm not sure but it looks like Carly might have used this getaway as an excuse to go shopping because she's wearing clothes I've never seen before. (Not that I pay attention to what Carly wears. Hel-lo.)

Matt and I make a last-minute run to the kitchen for snacks.

"We've already got fruit and water bottles in the car," Mom calls after us. "We're going to Malibu, not Madagascar!"

"But what if we get lost or stranded?" I argue.

stranded

Matt is quick to back me up. "Or if aliens invade before we get there and vaporize the earth's food supply?"

Mom rolls her eyes and tells us to hurry up.

vaporize

According to Dad's driving app, the beach house is only forty minutes away, but with Los Angeles traffic, forty minutes could mean

granola

clementines

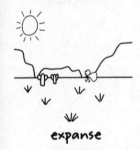

expanse

two hours—which is WAY too long to go without snacks. We throw a few more handfuls of granola bars, clementines, and string cheese into a bag and head to the car.

On the drive, Carly talks to my mom about her veterinary practice while Matt, Umberto, and I try to find the funniest GIFs. Umberto is definitely the winner with his *Game of Thrones/Walking Dead* mash-up.

But we all put down our phones as soon as the ocean comes into view. The expanse of beach in Santa Monica is so wide and bright, it always takes my breath away. People are rollerblading, power-walking, flying kites, playing volleyball, and swimming with plenty of room for everyone.

"We can go to the arcade at the pier if you kids get bored this weekend," Dad says.

"I'm not leaving the house," Mom says. "Reading magazines by the pool is the only thing on my agenda."

agenda

It takes another twenty minutes of driving to reach the turnoff. Even though the house is near the beach, it's tucked into the canyon, among hills and trees. The smell of jasmine— same as in my own backyard— surrounds me as soon as I step out of the car.

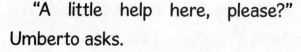

surrounds

"A little help here, please?" Umberto asks.

My parents hurry to retrieve Umberto's chair and help him out of the SUV. When we're all out, we take stock of the house in front of us.

It's the largest house I've ever seen.

"It's a mansion!" Carly says. "A glass castle!"

Mom's already typing the

passcode

aerial

passcode into the electronic lock on the door.

Inside, the ceilings are so high that the first thing I wonder is how the owners change the light bulbs. Do they have to call the fire department to bring in one of those aerial ladders? Or is there a jetpack in the hall closet? (Which would be great!)

"Oh good, you're here." A young woman in pink corduroys and a crop top waves from across the hall. "I'm Poufy's doggy nanny. You must be the veterinarian Darcy's been raving about!"

Mom shakes the woman's hand and introduces herself but all I'm thinking is, what kind of person gets a nanny just for their dog? The owner has only been away since this morning!

"I love your pants," Carly says to the young woman. "Can we meet Poufy now?"

"Poufy is in her wing of the house," the doggy nanny says. "I just gave her a post-brunch massage and tucked her into the warming bed with one of her playlists. She should be done meditating in about thirty minutes."

meditating

"She gets massages?" I ask.

"And meditates?" Matt adds. "How does that even work?"

"Yes, siree," the doggy nanny replies. "She is one balanced Pomeranian."

Pomeranian

Matt, Umberto, and I make eye contact and I know we're all thinking the same thing—this dog sounds RIDICULOUS.

The nanny reaches into her

messenger

messenger bag and pulls out a thick binder full of color-coded tabs. "This has everything you need to know about maintaining Poufy's schedule and social media presence."

"She's a dog," Matt blurts. "What kind of schedule could she possibly have?"

The doggy nanny laughs politely and explains that Poufy is "somewhat of an Instagram celebrity." Apparently Poufy is a model for a pet clothing and accessory company and actually gets paid to post pictures wearing their new designs.

She holds up her phone and shows us several thumbnails of a tiny butterscotch fuzzball in various tiaras and tutus.

"CUTE!" Carly nearly knocks me

over as she sticks her head between me and the young woman's phone. "What's her username? I'm totally following her."

"Princess_Poufy," the doggy nanny replies. She asks Mom for her phone number. "I'm texting you Poufy's log-in information. For the next few days, you'll be responsible for posting on Poufy's behalf."

chimes

Mom's phone chimes in her hand. Seconds later, my own phone sounds off with an incoming message. It's from Mom; she's already forwarded Poufy's Instagram log-in to me.

I hope this doesn't mean what I think it means.

"Derek will be in charge of the social media stuff." Mom smiles.

"ME?" I scramble for a way to get out of spending precious vacation time playing doggy dress-up with a spoiled Pomeranian. "Why can't Carly do it? She's already following Poufy anyway."

"What? Just because I'm a girl, I want to manage Poufy's posts?" Carly jokes. "No thanks."

There goes my exit strategy.

The doggy nanny switches her focus to me and goes through Poufy's posting protocol. "Twice a day on weekdays and three times Saturday and Sunday. Make sure Poufy's whole body is in frame and shoot from her level. No bird's-eye views."

Mom can tell that I'm about to be overwhelmed by the amount of info and steps in. "I think we can handle it from here. Thanks so much."

I give Mom a look in order to

protocol

communicate my appreciation. I haven't even MET this dog yet and I'm already working for her?

"One last thing," the nanny adds. "Set an alarm twenty-eight minutes from now. That's when you can rouse Poufy and refresh her water. There's a new pitcher in the fridge."

rouse

"Finally, we can get acquainted with the place," Dad says when the doggy nanny leaves.

I lift the enormous binder of instructions and thumb through the tabs. The grooming section alone is over twenty pages. "There's a different hairstyle for every day of the week?" I exclaim. "This is insane!"

grooming

Mom is too busy exploring Darcy's kitchen to answer. She runs her hand along the granite counters. "You could fit our whole house in this kitchen!

palatial

interior

I've never stayed anywhere so palatial!"

The entire interior of the house is white: walls, couches, tables, and chairs. The person who owns this house either never had kids or the kids are robots who barely move. Don't get me wrong, this is easily the greatest place I've ever stayed. But what's the point of having a huge house only to fill it with stuff that's WHITE?

Matt, Umberto, and Carly are as blown away as I am.

Carly posts several pictures on Snapchat and Instagram. Umberto zips through the wide rooms in his wheelchair until he skids to a halt.

"GUYS. This house has an elevator!" he shouts. "That's it; I'm moving in!"

I've never been in a house with an elevator, but imagine if the house had an escalator instead? As much fun as THAT would be, an elevator is obviously a much better choice, especially for Umberto.

escalator

Mom unpacks groceries while Dad pours them each a glass of wine. My friends and I take the elevator upstairs to the floor with the bedrooms. With six different ones to choose from, we each get our own room—and bathroom.

"This friend of your mom's must be a billionaire," Matt says. "You think your mom can borrow the house again in March so I can have my birthday here?"

billionaire

I tell him the person who owns the house is not really one of my mother's friends but one of her patients. What I don't tell him is that if she ever gets to borrow the house again, it'll be for MY birthday, not Matt's.

When we head back downstairs, Dad announces he's found something else: a screening room with cushy reclining chairs, each with their own tray and cup holder.

reclining

"Talk about extravagant," he says. "I can only imagine what the backyard is like!"

He opens the floor-to-ceiling glass door and we enter a large yard surrounded by mountains and wildflowers. Mom is already out there, admiring the landscaping and the view of the ocean. All I can think about is how many points I've scored with my friends without doing a thing.

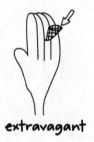

extravagant

landscaping

The outdoor furniture is also

white so I'm thinking this person DEFINITELY can't have kids—but then I see a twenty-foot rock-climbing wall, a trampoline, and an Olympic-sized swimming pool with a waterfall and a curly slide.

Let the long weekend begin!

PRINCESS POUFY

I'M RUNNING ACROSS THE YARD, when the alarm on my phone goes off.

Carly claps her hands. "Time to meet Poufy!"

"How has it been half an hour already?" Umberto rolls his wheel-chair reluctantly toward the house.

"This won't take long," I tell my friends as we ride the elevator to

Poufy's wing. "We'll check on the dog and be doing cannonballs into the pool in no time."

When we reach the second floor, we step into a hallway that looks like the trophy room at school. Along the walls are first-place awards and framed certificates from cities all around the world.

certificates

Matt and I press our faces against the display case to read the tiny plaque under a statue of a golden poodle. *Best in Show, West Coast Society of Canine Cuties: Princess Poufy.*

canine

Maybe it's just me, but I think there's something creepy about turning your dog into a beauty queen.

We reach Poufy's room, and I knock on the door.

Matt laughs. "You realize you're knocking on the door to a DOG'S room, right?"

"How's she supposed to open it?" Carly giggles.

I roll my eyes and open the door.

The first thing we notice is the sound of crashing waves and gentle piano music coming from speakers embedded in the ceiling. The second thing is the miniature princess canopy bed in the center of the room with a furry face peeking out from a pile of ruffled satin pillows.

"Hi, Poufy," I say with a small wave.

"She's so fluffy!" Carly gasps. Before I know it, she's sitting on the edge of Poufy's bed and petting her.

"Are you sure that's a dog?" Matt asks. "Looks more like a stuffed animal."

"Don't listen to them," Carly whispers in Poufy's ear. "I think you're precious."

"That creature can't be real," Umberto says. "She looks like a plushie of the cutest dog that ever lived."

I take a moment to examine the artwork on Poufy's walls. Hanging against a backdrop of pink-and-white-striped wallpaper are several paintings of dogs picking flowers, frolicking across hillsides, and riding in a gondola under the moonlight.

frolicking

Poufy hops out of Carly's arms and scampers over to a low table set with cups, saucers, and a tall pitcher. She nudges the bowl in front of her and lets out two happy yaps.

gondola

"No way." Matt shakes his head.

"I am NOT sitting down to a tea party with a dog."

"Not dressed like that you aren't." Carly sifts through Poufy's closet and pulls out a blue doggy dress with flowers and holds it up to Matt. "These gardenias really bring out your eyes," she laughs.

gardenia

I poke my head into Poufy's closet and can't believe how jam-packed it is. Not only are there racks of dresses, but a whole shelf of hats, head-bands, sweaters, and several colors of rainboots in sets of four.

"Dogs aren't supposed to wear clothes," I say. "It's just wrong."

Umberto puts a hand over his mouth. "You've been letting Bodi run around naked for years!"

Carly hangs the dress back in the closet. "Didn't the nanny say Poufy was a model?"

"That's right, Derek," Matt teases. "Poufy's followers might spontaneously combust if they don't get a photo of her having tea soon."

combust

"Yeah, hurry up so we can go back to the pool," Umberto adds.

He's got a point; we've already spent way too much time inside. I snap a quick picture of Poufy perched on her chair next to the tea set.

"Looks good to me," Matt says, looking over my shoulder.

Suddenly Poufy jumps onto the table and places her front paws on my stomach. She yaps and stands on her hind legs, trying to knock my phone out of my hands with her nose.

"Down, Poufy!" I say, but she won't take her eyes off it. "Why is she trying to eat my phone?" I just got the screen fixed and it cost me

HOURS of chores around the house. If it breaks while we're here, Mom might make me clean the whole mansion.

"It says in Poufy's manual that she likes to review the photos of herself before she posts them," Carly says.

There's no way I heard that right. "She posts them herself?"

"A dog that can use an iPhone?" Umberto blurts. "Now I've seen everything!"

"She *technically* posts them herself. Really, she just hits share with her nose." Carly closes the binder, looking pleased with herself. "Another example of when reading instructions comes in handy."

"Makes no difference to me." I hold out my phone in front of

Poufy's face and she instantly taps the share button with her little wet nose.

"There." I slide my phone back into my pocket. "Last one in the pool is a rotten egg!"

But as soon as I swing open the door, I notice my mother's making her way upstairs with a pitcher of water in one hand and her phone in the other.

"Darcy just texted and said you didn't use any of Poufy's hashtags in the photo you posted." Mom's phone chimes with another incoming text message, and she glances down to read it. "Page thirty-seven of the manual."

"She's right." Carly shows me a couple of Princess_Poufy's previous posts on her phone. "#princesslife;

#Poufy, #puppylove, #dogmodel. There are at least a dozen hashtags on each photo."

"I came to Malibu to be on VACATION." I turn to Carly and give her some puppy-dog eyes of my own. "Can't you handle Poufy's Instagram for the weekend?" I plead. "You're the one who thinks she's cute."

immune

Carly remains immune to my pleas. "I'm a guest, remember? Poufy is *your* responsibility."

"She's right." Mom thrusts Poufy's manual into my hands. I swear there are even more pages in it now than when I first looked at it an hour ago. "There will definitely be plenty of time to enjoy the perks of the mansion, but Poufy is our primary responsibility."

teeters

Matt teeters from heel to toe with

an anxious grin on his face. "Does that mean the rest of us can go swimming?"

Instead of answering him, Mom does that thing where she stares me down and waits for me to make the right decision on my own.

"Go ahead," I sigh. "I'll be out in a minute."

"Yahoo!" Umberto leads the way and my friends head off to enjoy the pool without me.

I glare at Poufy; I thought humans were supposed to be a dog's master, not the other way around.

She trots over and wags her fuzz-ball of a tail. "Yes, I know," I groan. "I'm adding the hashtags now."

I take a seat on the carpet and pat her head. The softness of her fur puts me in a slightly better mood and I see Mom's point. Even though I think it's insane for a dog to be modeling clothes, it means I get to stay in this stunning beach house with my friends for the long weekend.

#lucky

A QUESTION OF TECHNOLOGY

WE SPEND THE NEXT FEW HOURS racing from the water slide to the climbing wall to the trampoline while my parents lounge by the pool with a giant stack of magazines between them. I can't fathom how anyone would choose to READ in a place with so many other cool things to do.

Matt and I are about to carry Umberto's wheelchair onto the

lounge

fathom

nixes

trampoline when Dad comes out in his grilling apron with a plate of burger patties and nixes our plan. He shoots me his Make-Good-Choices face before he turns on the grill.

School's still in session but this sure feels like summer vacation. I wonder if the person who lives here feels like they're on vacation all year long.

marvels

After lunch, Matt suggests we take a break from all the physical activity and head inside to game. While Dad marvels at how gigantic the TV is, Matt, Umberto, and I tally up all the gaming systems: Play-Station, Nintendo, Xbox, even a vintage Atari—all loaded with the latest games, just waiting to be played.

Matt leaps into one of the comfy leather armchairs facing the screen.

"Can you believe these seats?" He presses the buttons on the side of the arm and the chair reclines while two cup holders and a footrest pop out.

"Let me see!" Umberto wheels over to the chair next to Matt and Dad helps him in while Carly sinks into an aisle seat.

Umberto leans back and closes his eyes. "This chair is like a vacation for my butt."

I'm about to take the last chair when Poufy prances past me and jumps onto the seat cushion.

"Scoot over, Poufy," I tell her.

But Poufy just circles the cushion and settles in.

"Sorry, Derek." Carly smiles. "Looks like that seat's taken."

I ignore her and gently try to

move Poufy onto the arm of the chair. "Come on, Poufy. There's plenty of room for both of us."

Umberto laughs. "I think Poufy disagrees."

"Careful, she might try to mark her territory," Matt adds, "and you'll have to clean it up."

I plop onto the floor determined not to let it bother me, but I can't help think this would NEVER happen with Bodi. My mutt is a billion times better behaved than this Instagram celebrity, hands down.

Even though I'm not a great student and reading is difficult, I've always considered myself good at other things like skateboarding, gaming, and figuring out how stuff works. So I'm kind of surprised when I can't decode the remote to the

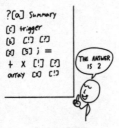

decode

giant TV. But that might be because the remote is half the size of my bed.

"One of these has to be the power button," Umberto says as he points to the remote.

But try as we might, none of us can get the TV to work. We're still a little worn out from an afternoon in the sun, so we relax and play games on our phones instead.

"I'm loving your stick figure memes," Umberto tells me. "A nice break from all the photos."

That's high praise from a kid whom I really respect as an artist. I thank him for the compliment.

Mom buzzes through the room and I can tell she's about to talk, then catches herself. She wants to give us grief for being on our phones but quickly realizes we're actually COMMUNICATING with one another. Trading memes and GIFs is our way of sharing a joke.

tortillas

She DOES make us put the phones away when it's time for dinner. The kitchen island—which is the size of an SUV—is full of all the fixings for tacos. Matt, Umberto, Carly, and I load our plates with chicken, fish, tortillas, salsa, guacamole, and sour cream and settle in for a feast.

Best. Weekend. Ever!

THE FIRST SIGN
OF TROUBLE

WHEN I COME DOWN TO BREAK-
fast the next morning, Carly is
already in the kitchen helping Dad
scoop watermelon and cantaloupe
into a giant bowl. The television
hanging from the kitchen cabinet is
turned on to the news.

cantaloupe

"A wildfire started last night in
the next canyon," Dad says. "We're
fine as long as the fire doesn't jump
the highway."

unstoppable

I try to imagine a fire so unstop-pable that it barrels down a freeway. For a moment I'm scared, until I look at the fire on TV—it's mostly smoke and only a little orange.

Suddenly Dad's phone starts buzz-ing. He wipes his hands on a dish towel and answers.

"It's Darcy," he mouths to me. "Yes, we saw the news...Sorry Carol didn't answer. I think she's outside. Poufy is excellent; she and Derek are getting along great."

That part is a bit of a stretch, but the last thing I want is to get roped into a lecture from Poufy's owner.

"We'll absolutely keep you posted." Dad puts down the phone and shakes his head. "How did Darcy get MY number?"

Carly follows me outside. As usual,

she reads my mind. "Darcy's probably just scared by the news report.
So, what should we do first?"

I always think it's funny when
grown-ups complain about having
too many options. Having too many
options is a GOOD thing. Choosing
between a pool, video game, rock
climbing, or trampoline is a nice problem to have—trust me.

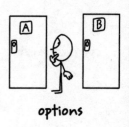

options

Mom's already outside on her
yoga mat in the middle of a sun salutation. When I tell her she missed a
call from Darcy, she hardly reacts.

salutation

"The wildfire's nowhere near us,"
Mom says with her toes high in the
air in a shoulder stand. "No need to
worry."

"Then I guess it's a good thing
I'm not," I answer.

I don't know if it's to suck up to

contortionist

her, but Carly puts down her bowl of fruit and starts doing yoga alongside my mom. When they ask me to join them, I say I never go contortionist on an empty stomach and head back inside.

Umberto and Matt have joined Dad at the TV. I'm shocked to see how much the fire has grown in the short time I've been outside.

"I'll keep an eye on this," Dad says. "You boys go have fun and don't worry about the fire."

Funny thing about people telling you not to worry—it makes you worry MORE.

I CAN GET USED TO THIS

YOU WANT US TO WHAT?!

MY FRIENDS AND I ARE TOO BUSY diving for quarters and toy gems in the pool to even think about what's going on with the wildfire. The Olympic-sized pool has a long bench built inside; between that and the many rafts, Umberto is able to fully enjoy himself too. He's also done lots of adaptive rock-climbing, so he rappels down the wall even faster than I do.

adaptive

rappels

When we head back into the house, Mom is pulling out a fresh loaf of banana bread. "This oven is spectacular," Mom says. "I just had to use it."

While I don't quite understand how anyone could get excited over an appliance, I'll never complain about baked goods. She cuts a small piece for us to taste, and Carly asks my mother for an update on the fire.

update

"The firefighters are working hard," Mom answers. "It should be under control by the end of the day." She then tells us we'll be leaving for the beach after she cooks Poufy's Saturday meal.

I nearly do a double take. "Cook? For the dog?"

"Darcy has her on a special weekend meal plan," Mom replies. "It's not

anything a veterinarian would prescribe, but it's what Darcy requested."

prescribe

I know she would never complain,
but I can tell from the tone of Mom's
voice that she's had about as much
as she can take of Poufy's crazy
regimen.

I don't want her to think I'm
neglecting my responsibilities with
Poufy, so I help cut up the chicken
livers and fresh thyme for Poufy's
breakfast. Even though it's probably
not in the manual, Mom makes a
few extra portions and puts them in
the fridge for later.

When all the food is portioned
and labeled, Mom smiles. "I think it's
time to get down to the ocean, don't
you?"

I tell her I couldn't agree more.

She dries her hands on a towel

and checks the time. "That's odd—the doggy nanny should've been here fifteen minutes ago." She picks up her phone and finds a voice mail. "It's from the nanny." She presses the phone to her ear and I can tell from her face that things just got worse.

"She's not coming." Mom frowns. "A power line landed in the street during the wildfire and she can't get out."

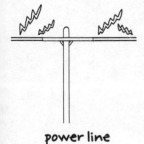

power line

"So we'll pack Poufy in a beach bag and take her with us." Even though I was looking forward to an afternoon where I didn't have to be at Poufy's beck and call, it's not the end of the world.

"That would be an option," Mom sighs. "But the beaches in Malibu don't allow dogs. Tell your father I'll be sitting this one out."

"That's not fair."

"Someone has to stay here and look after Poufy." Mom kisses the top of my head and tells me to have fun.

Matt, Umberto, Carly, and I grab our beach towels and sunblock, then meet Dad at the car. We hang out the windows and wave to Mom and Poufy as we make our way down the long driveway.

I know *someone* had to stay behind with Poufy—and I'm glad it wasn't me—but keeping Mom from enjoying the beach docks Poufy a few more points in my book. Although I can't help but wonder if Mom is secretly glad she gets to have the mansion to herself while we're gone.

When I go to the beach with my parents, we mostly head to El Matador

rickety

kiosk

with its beautiful stone-sculpture cliffs made from centuries of wind and water. But the only way down is a long set of rickety stairs; it is definitely NOT handicap accessible. Before I can take Dad aside to ask about Umberto, he shows us a photo on his phone of the wheelchairs they have at the main beach near the pier. The chairs have giant balloon tires that make it easy for them to move on sand. I feel better knowing Umberto will be able to enjoy the beach as much as the activities at the house.

Dad treats us to lunch at a local clam shack where it takes us longer to wait in line than it does to eat our food. The college girl at the beach-wheelchair kiosk is really nice; Carly sees the novel she's reading and ends up talking to her about her favorite beach reads. She tries to rope me into the conversation, but the ocean is beckoning, so I tell her I'm going to find a place to lay out our blanket.

beckoning

Dad offers to wheel Umberto down to the water but Umberto's in the middle of a graphic novel and wants to sit under the umbrella in the new chair and finish it. Carly offers to keep him company while Matt, Dad, and I race to the water.

The Pacific is as warm as I've ever felt it, so we stay in until we're exhausted from riding and jumping waves. As we make our way back to the blanket, we spot Carly wheeling Umberto along the shoreline chasing seagulls. I take some quick videos with my phone to show them later.

grumpy

fantasizing

dribble

It takes us forever to pack up our stuff at the end of the day. When we finally get back to the wheelchair kiosk to return the one with special tires, the nice college girl who chatted with Carly has been replaced by a grumpy old lady who practically throws Umberto's wheelchair into the return area. On the way back, we stop for ice cream in giant waffle cones even though it's almost time for dinner.

"I love fantasizing that we live here," Matt says. "Do you think if I got a job scooping ice cream down the street, Darcy would let me rent a room in her mansion?"

"Yes, especially with how much ice cream you'd spill on that white furniture." Carly points to the dribble of melted chocolate where Matt is sitting.

Dad definitely overheard Carly's comment, because when we get back to the beach house, he makes me and Matt clean the backseat with soap and warm water and vacuum out the sand too.

I'm on my way to change clothes when I spot Mom and Dad in the kitchen shaking their heads.

Mom points to the TV. "The wildfire just jumped the highway. The fire's heading our way."

My eyes are fixed to the carpet of orange flames tearing up a nearby canyon.

"Tell your friends to pack after they shower," Dad continues. "We're going home."

"What? We can't leave!" I argue. "We haven't had enough fun yet!"

My parents aren't buying my argument; it's time to change course.

"What about Poufy?" She's the last of my concerns, but I know Mom and Dad would never bail on an agreement they made with a friend.

"I spoke to Darcy," Mom begins, "who agrees it's best if we take Poufy home with us."

NOOOOOOOO!

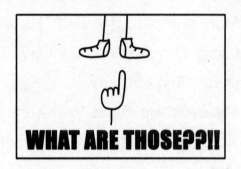

WHAT ARE THOSE??!!

IT GETS WORSE

CARLY AND UMBERTO TAKE THE news pretty well; Matt and I are the ones who don't want to leave.

"The wildfire is still miles away," I tell my parents.

"Firefighters from all over the state are here," Matt adds. "They'll definitely put it out."

"It's scorched a thousand acres so far," Dad says. "Plus we live less

scorched

than an hour away. It's not like we flew three thousand miles to vacation here. It's the smart thing to do."

Matt and I exchange looks. Neither of us could ever be accused of making the smart choice the first time around.

Mom agrees with Dad. "Better safe than sorry. I'm sure Darcy will let us use the house again."

She makes sure my friends have all texted their parents to let them know they're safe and will be home a few days early.

Carly scrolls through her own Instagram page. "At least we have a lot of pictures to remember our vacation by."

I'm about to tell her that photographs hardly compare to the real thing, when there's a loud knock at the front door.

"Who can that be?" Mom asks no one in particular.

When she opens the door, a man and woman in uniforms are outside. They hold up badges and say they're from the Malibu Sheriff's Department.

uniforms

"If this is about the wildfire," Dad begins, "we're on our way back to Westwood."

"This IS about the fire," the man says. "But you won't be heading to Westwood. Another power line's down and the PCH is closed."

In all the years I've lived here, I've never heard of the Pacific Coast Highway being blocked. I didn't even think it was possible.

"We can take the canyon road to the 101," Mom says.

The policewoman shakes her head. "I'm afraid that's where the wildfire

warning

is most dangerous. We've had to close the 101 on this side of the canyon."

I assume these officers are going house to house warning people about the roads, which just goes to show Malibu really is the small town that people who live here say it is. "If the road is closed, that means we can stay here instead of going home!" I tell my parents. "This is GOOD news."

evacuate

"Actually you CAN'T stay," the policewoman says. "That's why we're here. You need to evacuate."

Matt nudges me like this is the excitement he's been waiting for.

"No problem," Dad says. "Even if it takes us three times as long, we'll be heading back home."

"That's what we're trying to tell

you." The officer with the mustache gestures toward the canyon behind him. "We're here to secure the area. Until the roads are safe, we're asking all residents to head to the evacuation center at the high school."

Mom shakes her head. "Thanks for your concern, but we live here in Los Angeles. We don't need to go to an evacuation center."

The man takes a step closer. "I'm afraid you do, ma'am. Please follow us down to the high school."

"We'd be happy to," Dad interrupts. "But we've got a dog with us."

"Not a problem," the female officer answers. "The evacuation center is set up for pets too."

Mom turns to Dad with an alarmed look on her face. "What am I going to tell Darcy?"

alarmed

I know I should probably also be concerned about what to do with Poufy, but Umberto, Matt, and I share a look that proves we're all thinking the same thing.

Getting evacuated = an unplanned adventure!

OOPS

MOM CONTINUES TO QUESTION the officers until Dad gives her a look to drop it. When it comes to dealing with authority figures, Dad's philosophy is to go with the flow instead of argue. It's always interesting to watch my parents deal with other people in the world who are in charge of them since they're usually the bosses—at least when it comes to me.

authority

precautions

reassures

Carly calls her mom, who wants to speak to MY mom. They chat about how the town is taking extra precautions to keep everyone safe and we'll probably be home in a few hours. Umberto's parents are out of town but Mom talks to his brother Eduardo and reassures him too. Matt's mom agrees with mine that evacuating the canyon seems unnecessary but she trusts that Matt will be fine with us.

"I guess there's no one left to call but Darcy," Mom sighs.

As excited as I am to see what getting evacuated will be like, I do feel bad that this stressful situation landed in Mom's lap. I break away from my friends to stand next to her while she waits for Darcy to pick up. We both smile when the call goes to voice mail.

"Hi," Mom begins. "Everything's fine, but we're being evacuated as a precaution. The fire is still miles away and Poufy will be traveling safely with us to the evacuation center." Mom gives Darcy the address we'll be at before she hangs up and tells me to make sure we have everything Poufy might need.

It takes me a while to gather all of Poufy's things—especially because Carly makes me triple-check everything on the "overnight travel essentials list" on page 42 of the instruction binder. With suitcases full of toys, outfits, and pillows, Poufy easily has twice the luggage of anyone else in the car.

I buckle Poufy into her car seat and take a photo of her wearing a pair of heart-shaped sunglasses for her Instagram account. Once I include all her hashtags, I hold my phone in front of her face for her approval.

"What do you think?"

Poufy juts her nose toward the screen and taps the share button. I have to admit, it's a pretty cool trick. If Poufy can learn how to share her own posts, I wonder if I could train Bodi to play Fortnite.

We load everything into the trunk and take one last look around the property—the best vacation house any of us has ever been in and now we have to leave.

As Dad routes the GPS to the evacuation center, Carly points out that a lot of TV and movie actors live in Malibu. If the whole area is evacuated, forget about camping under the stars, we'll be camping WITH the stars. The excitement of rubbing elbows with our favorite celebrities skids to a halt, however, when we round a corner on the exit detour and come face-to-face with a wall of orange flames in what used to be the hillside.

detour

"It's ... gone." Matt's mouth hangs open even after he's done talking.

I've seen fires on the news before, but they didn't prepare me for seeing the destruction of a natural disaster firsthand.

When we get to the high school, the cops escort us in—probably to ensure that Mom doesn't jump back in the car and try to head home, which she might've done if we hadn't just seen the hills ablaze.

escort

"Maybe all the food will be in cans,"

Matt says as we enter the gym, "and we'll have to open them with a knife 'cuz they forgot can openers."

"And they only have beans," Umberto adds. "So the gym becomes totally filled with farts."

"OMG," I realize. "Everyone knows farts are flammable. If the wildfires reach us, we'll be doomed!"

Carly holds her phone above her head and walks around the gym. "Not to burst your bubble, but there's no cell service here."

"WHAT???"

This news might be worse than having to leave the beach house.

A woman unpacking jugs of water agrees. "Service went down an hour ago. There's no Wi-Fi either. Hopefully they'll be up by tomorrow."

TOMORROW?

"This IS a disaster!" I say.

"That sentence is literally true," Carly adds. "Our phones are pretty much useless."

"No texts, no memes, no apps, no NOTHING!" Matt panics.

All six of us move our cell phones through the air as if there's a magic spot where there IS service. But the woman is right; it's definitely down.

I lift Poufy's crate to eye level. "Sorry, Poufy—looks like this will put a damper on your Instagram schedule."

"Is that PRINCESS POUFY?" A girl a few years older than me runs over. When she gets a close look at Poufy, she squeals and calls over her friends. "Melody! Erica! Guess who's here!"

FALL
APART

literally

swarm

Suddenly I'm surrounded by a swarm of tween girls, shrieking and cooing at Poufy. (I'd rather they were shrieking and cooing at me, but I'll take whatever attention from these girls I can get.)

"I've been following her all year!" one of them tells me. "Are you her owner?"

I smile and tell her I'm watching Poufy for the weekend.

"I saw that post of Princess Poufy buckled into her car seat just before the service went out," another Poufy fan gushes. "I NEVER would've guessed she was on her way to this evacuation center!"

I debate telling them that Poufy actually shared that post herself but decide not to because it sounds ridiculous. Instead, I ask the girls if they also follow the meme site that my friends and I use.

When the girls leave, Dad laughs and tells me in a few more years I'll probably be begging to borrow Poufy. "That dog might be a royal pain, but she certainly is a chick magnet," he says.

I make Dad promise to throw me off a cliff if I ever try to use Poufy to meet girls. (Although it DID seem to work.)

When we find Mom, she's next in line at the Red Cross station. A woman who introduces herself as Marika shows us where the rest-rooms and cafeteria are. She then walks us over to where the bleachers are folded up against the wall. "Once you pick out your cots, this will be your slice of home for the night."

bleachers

Mom shakes her head. "We live just a few towns away. We won't be here overnight."

The woman smiles as if she knows something we don't. "You can pick up pillows and blankets in the hall."

Dad's antennae tell him Mom's about to fly into panic mode, so he claps his hands together as if this is all part of the weekend activities. "If—and I mean IF—we have to stay the night, it'll be an adventure, right, kids?"

sleepover

Carly picks up on his idea and joins in. "Like a sleepover. We can have a séance!"

séance

"WE'RE NOT HAVING A SÉANCE!" Matt shouts. "We're exploring and eating beans and getting into trouble."

"Technically séances ARE exploring and getting into trouble," Carly
responds.

I'd never admit it to anyone, but
I'm impressed Carly can still be her
sassy self in the middle of an
emergency.

sassy

"There'll be time for all those
things," Dad says. "Right, Carol?" He
looks to my mom with a pleading
face.

"Absolutely," she finally says.
"Let's make the best of it."

Mom's obviously adjusted her
thinking because she tells Marika
she's a veterinarian and can help out
with any animal medical needs if
necessary.

"We can pretend we're in high
school and we GO here," Carly says.
"That'll be fun."

Matt shakes his head like his brain is short-circuiting. "Why would we pretend we're in school on a WEEKEND?!"

surveillance

He turns to me and Umberto, and we follow him down the hall to do some surveillance.

NOT COOL

BUT WE'RE IN
A GYM!

MOM HAS POUFY SAFE IN HER
crate and is waiting for a cell signal
so she can text Darcy we're settled
and everything's okay, which means
I'm off the hook for a while. Carly
decides to stay with Poufy but
Umberto, Matt, and I are determined to explore. Luckily the school's
on one floor with wide hallways, so
Umberto can maneuver easily with
his wheelchair.

suppress

retrace

"Is it my imagination or are there twice as many people now than when we got here?" I ask.

Umberto agrees. "The roads must still be closed. I hope they suppress the fire soon."

As we turn the corner, we come face-to-face with a man with a clipboard and headset. "You kids need to get back to the gym. The school isn't a playground."

We turn and retrace our steps. "Thanks for telling us a school isn't a playground," Matt whispers. "As if we had them confused."

"Was this door open before?" I point to the band room, full of instruments.

"Somebody must've just opened it." Umberto wheels into the room with me and Matt right behind him.

The room is set up with curved rows of folding chairs, just like a regular orchestra. I grab a pencil from my back pocket and pretend to conduct invisible musicians. Matt immediately jumps in and starts banging on the drum set in the corner.

orchestra

"They have a timpani!" Umberto exclaims. "My favorite type of drum!" He starts banging on the kettledrum alongside Matt.

timpani

The only thing I know about how a conductor conducts is that he waves his arms, which I'm now doing like a madman. How Umberto and Matt are supposed to interpret my movements is beyond me. And based on Matt's and Umberto's random banging, it's beyond them too.

interpret

"WHAT ON EARTH IS GOING ON IN HERE?"

The man with the clipboard and headset stands in the doorway, furious. Matt and Umberto stop playing while my arms remain frozen in midair.

"An evacuation is a serious matter," the man says. "Several families might lose their homes and you three are acting like you're at summer camp." He extends his arm and points down the hall. "Go back to the gym and stay there. NOW."

The man doesn't have to ask twice; the three of us hightail it out of the room before he's finished talking.

"I guess he won't be asking for an encore," I whisper as we hurry away.

The three of us laugh as we escape—until we turn the corner. The giant window facing us shows a

encore

view of the canyon from the other side of the building.

"Is that . . . snow?" Matt asks.

I shake my head. I'm guessing it's never snowed in Malibu. "That's ash," I answer. "From the fire."

My friends and I are speechless as we watch the cinders drift across the sky. "It's like someone emptied a giant pencil sharpener," Matt finally says.

cinders

Umberto shakes his head. "Maybe the guy in the band room was right. Maybe what's happening is more serious than we thought."

I'm still without words as I stare at the sky in awe and sadness.

WORST. SLEEPOVER.

EVER!

WE TRY TO HELP

WHEN WE FIND MY PARENTS, THE look on Dad's face tells me the news isn't good.

"Both roads in and out are closed, so we're here for the night." When he raises his eyebrows and looks at me, I know he's hoping I won't freak out and make things worse.

"I'm just worried about Bodi," I tell him. I look over at Poufy happily

lapping up the organic chicken-liver-
and-pea pâté Mom made for her
earlier and can't help but miss my
own faithful canine. I wonder how
Bodi's holding up without us. Does
he know we're on the outskirts of
danger?

pâté

Dad turns to my friends. "When
we get service, you kids should
text your parents to let them know
we're remaining here until the fire
subsides."

remaining

I've gone to plenty of sleepovers
but never one where I slept on a mili-
tary cot next to a hundred strangers.
Part of me is excited to be doing
something new while another part is
worried and just wants to go home.

My parents know me well enough
to realize I'll need to keep busy so I
don't spiral out of control. Dad grabs

his bag with his sketchbook and pencils and tells me to come along. He pulls over a bench in the corner of the gym and sketches a quick sign that says CARICATURES.

"This is good practice for you too," he tells me. "Anytime there's an opportunity to draw, you should take it."

wandering

There are so many people wandering around trying to figure out what to do that offering to draw their portraits seems like a good idea. I dig my own pencils out of my bag and take a seat beside him.

offering

"Who wants to be our first guinea pig?" Dad calls into the gym. "Who's interested in a free caricature?"

We're suddenly surrounded by a group of local kids, each of them a million times cooler than I am. With their board shorts and gnarled hair, I'm guessing they're surfers who live nearby.

gnarled

While Dad sketches, he asks the first kid to tell us a little about himself.

"My name's Oliver," the boy says. "I live on the beach and don't want to be here."

"None of us do," I say.

He whips his head around to face me. "The waves are killer today—this whole evacuation is a nightmare."

I nod like I agree, even though I've only surfed once in my life. I add the word *totally* for good measure.

When Dad hands him his caricature, Oliver lets out a giant "Whoa!!" He holds the drawing in front of his face like a mask and does a rambunctious dance.

rambunctious

revel

Dad doesn't revel in the fact that his drawing is good; instead, he merely motions for another kid to sit down and be his next subject. I wish I was as confident as Dad with my own drawing skills. I just hope that's something that will come in time.

I look around the gym to find my friends but the only one I can see is Matt, hanging around the food area looking to score more snacks. He sees me checking him out and pulls two chocolate bars from the front pocket of his sweatshirt.

Sorry, Dad. I'd love to stay but candy's calling.

GANGNAM STYLE

GRIM NEWS

AFTER MATT AND I TAKE A LAP around the food stations, we return to our cots to stash our plunder of peanut butter crackers and fruit gummies.

Mom puts down her book as soon as she sees me. "Next shift is yours." She stands and grabs her purse. "I'm going to stretch my legs."

I don't have to ask what she's referring to.

Poufy duty.

I peer through the crate to see Poufy asleep on her crown-shaped pillow. She's still wearing her tiara. The older girls from earlier quietly take pictures of Poufy as she sleeps.

Matt collapses facedown on a cot and lets out an exaggerated groan. "Why does time always go by so much slower when you're in a school?"

"They should have tried to figure that out on an episode of *MythBusters*—to see if all schools are built in time-warp zones."

Carly interrupts our complaining and tells us to join her at the center of the gym. I grab Poufy's crate and drag her with us to where Carly's assembled a group of toddlers.

"I don't know what you have in

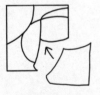

assembled

mind, but we're not hanging out with three-year-olds," I tell her.

She rolls her eyes, then addresses the circle of kids. "Welcome to story time," she says. "I brought along two special guests."

Matt and I exchange glances. Carly can't possibly mean US.

"Actually make that THREE!"

Before I can stop her, Carly opens Poufy's carrier and lifts Poufy up for the toddlers to see. Their attention is like a spotlight that wakes Poufy from her slumber.

"Doggy!" a few of them shout.

"That's right," Carly says. "Everyone say hello to Princess Poufy."

Carly sits the Pomeranian in her lap and a chorus of kid voices greet Princess Poufy. I silently hope none of them get the urge to touch Poufy's

savanna

fur with their sticky hands—not because I think Poufy won't like it but because I'm sure somehow from the African savanna Darcy will sense something's amiss and fire off a flurry of angry texts to my mom.

Luckily, the toddlers stay seated as Carly asks them what book they'd like to read.

"*Goodnight Moon!*" shouts a little girl.

"Great choice!" Carly turns to me. "You want to start, Derek?"

The thing is, *Goodnight Moon* was one of my favorite books when I was little—it was one of the only ones I could read by myself—but sitting here surrounded by three-year-olds with expectant faces stops me in my tracks. Can't we go back to the band room and bang on the drums again?

"Okay, everybody take a seat," Carly continues. "Crisscross applesauce."

This time Matt's the one who rolls his eyes. "You've been waiting since preschool to say that," he tells Carly. "I'm out of here."

Carly grabs my arm before I can escape. "Derek LOVES this book. Right, Derek?"

And just like that, I find myself surrounded by a dozen little kids looking up at me with keen expressions. I grab the book from Carly's hand; the faster I get this over with, the better.

keen

"*Goodnight Moon*," I begin. "In the great green room, there was a telephone—"

"You're reading it wrong," a boy with teeth the size of Tic Tacs says.

It's a complaint I've heard my entire life, but this is the first time I've heard it from a little kid.

"I am NOT reading it wrong," I say. "Besides, I'm only a few words in!"

"It's not the words," the boy says. "You have to do the voices!"

A few of the other kids join in. "Do funny voices!"

"And hold Poufy while you read it!" another little girl shouts.

The only thing more ridiculous than their requests is the smile on Carly's face as she places the Pomeranian on my lap. She is LOVING this.

"Funny voices it is." I start with a Donald Duck impersonation that even I can't understand, followed by SpongeBob and Cookie Monster.

Bond. James Bond

impersonation

The kids listen and laugh with rapt attention. This might be the first time I've read aloud where I'm not crawling back to my seat in embarrassment. I don't even lose my place when I sneeze mid-sentence. I'm actually feeling pretty good about myself—until I look up and spot that surfer Oliver pointing his phone at me.

"Posting a picture?" I ask him. "#evacuation?"

He shakes his head. "Taking a video of a grown kid reading *Goodnight Moon* to a dog in a tiara."

rebuke

Before I can rebuke him, Carly jumps in and says we're helping to keep the little kids entertained.

"This is DEFINITELY entertaining," Oliver says. "Especially when I make it a meme."

"You make memes too?" I ask. "So do we."

But Oliver doesn't seem interested in our mutual hobby and takes off.

"Just ignore him," Carly says.

I feel the same frustration and confusion I felt when I first met Umberto. Given how much we both loved to draw, we should've been friends from day one. Instead we butted heads for a long time before realizing we actually had a lot of things in common. I hate the awkwardness that can happen when you meet someone new.

awkwardness

A little while later my phone dings; we have service! I get a text from Matt who's obviously been on Instagram. He forwards me an attachment and I gasp when I see it. It's a meme of me that must've been taken while I was sneezing because my face is scrunched up in a way that makes it look like I'm crying. Poufy sitting on my lap in her tiara is plainly visible. The text above and below my face says:

visible

A DIFFERENT KIND
OF DISASTER

insulted

IT'S NOT LIKE THIS IS THE FIRST time I've been made fun of. It's not even the first time I've been insulted in a meme. (Thanks, Matt. Thanks, Umberto. Thanks, Carly.) But it's also not every day you're ridiculed by someone you barely know.

"Going back to the classics, Derek?" Matt asks. "You always DID like *Goodnight Moon*, or should I say, *Goodnight Meme*."

I tell him he's making things worse.

"Get over it," he says. "We put people in memes all the time."

"Not REAL people," I answer.

"Leonardo DiCaprio is a real person. So is Keanu Reeves—and you've made dozens of memes using them."

"They're MOVIE STARS! They're OLD! Not a random twelve-year-old trying to read to little kids."

random

Matt laughs. "So you admit you were TRYING to read—not actually reading. *Goodnight Moon* still giving you trouble?"

I don't bother responding, I just look through the gym to find Oliver and give him a piece of my mind—an idea I'm committed to until I finally find him.

responding

I look him in the eye and gather

up my strength. "What's your problem?" I finally ask. "You know I was
helping keep those kids busy so
they don't run around making a
nuisance."

nuisance

"That's funny 'cuz that's what
I'M trying to do—be the biggest
nuisance possible."

"Mission accomplished." I take
another deep breath and ask the
REALLY important question. "Can
you please take down that meme?"

Oliver tugs at his messy hair and
tells me that's not going to happen.
Just as I'm about to ask again, I look
behind him at two of the other boys
who were with him earlier. One's
wearing a trucker hat from the
eighties, the other has on so many
layered T-shirts that his sleeves are
four different color stripes.

layered

"No one's going to see it anyway," I tell Oliver. "You only have forty-six followers."

Oliver shrugs and points to the kid in the trucker hat. "That may be true, but Brian has four thousand seven hundred and fifty." His finger swipes across the screen of his phone. "We'll see what happens now that HE has it."

"Same thing that happened when you had it: nothing. The meme isn't good enough to get any traction."

"You might be right," Oliver says. "We should've looked for a more interesting subject."

I turn around to see Matt a few feet away. He must notice how angry I am, because he jogs over after Oliver leaves. "Hey, at least they didn't add Poufy's hashtag—with

traction

how many followers SHE has, that meme would've gotten a lot more views."

I'm about to tell him he's right, when Brian whips around with a huge grin. "Thanks for the tip, dude!"

Matt looks at me nervously. "Oops."

The smoke coming out of my ears inspires me to find Mom and ask for an update on the fire. I need to get out of this gym ASAP.

"The PCH is still closed," she says. "Once it opens tomorrow we can go home."

I ask her if the roads near our house are passable.

"Don't worry," she says. "If we can't get home, we'll go to a hotel."

Right now, the only thing on

my mind is the comfort of home. I miss my room, my yard, and, most of all, my dog. As if she knows what I'm thinking, Mom tells me she just talked to Cindy who said Bodi is fine.

Mom's phone chimes again. "Really? I just spoke with you five minutes ago." She shakes her head as she types a reply on her screen. "Darcy's worried sick about Poufy. My phone's almost dead; I'm going to the charging station."

I follow her gaze to the long line of people standing against the wall. "All those people are waiting to charge their phones?"

Mom nods. "I heard they're kicking you off the outlets as soon as your battery gets to twenty percent."

I spot Carly and Umberto near the front of the line and hurry toward them. "How long did you guys have to wait?" I ask.

"Forty minutes," Umberto says.

"Worse than a doctor's appointment," Carly adds.

The woman holding a baby behind Umberto pipes up. "That's how long I've been waiting too. I hope you don't think you're cutting in." She lowers her head and stares at me over her glasses.

Of course I was trying to cut—two of my best friends are next!

bore

The woman continues to bore her eyes into me. The baby stares too, as well as the people behind her. I shuffle to the back of the line, thirty-nine people behind Carly and Umberto.

My phone and Mom's will definitely be dead by the time we get to
the front. It hardly matters, though,
'cuz I've got nothing else to do.
Nothing.

LIGHTS OUT

EVEN THOUGH MY FRIENDS AND I have been eating pretty much non-stop, when it's dinnertime we race to the cafeteria to eat.

While we stand in line, Mom apologizes to my friends again. But Matt, Carly, and Umberto seem fine with the surprise sleepover.

"It'll be like that time we stayed overnight at the zoo on that field trip a few years ago," Matt says.

"Except this time, WE'RE the ones in a cage," I say. "Suppose we have to stay all weekend?"

"More than a million and a half people were evacuated for Hurricane Katrina," Carly says. "Hopefully we won't get that many people here."

It feels like there ARE that many people in the gym. I can tell it's gotten more crowded just based on how difficult it is for Umberto to maneuver around. When I think about how much worse this must be for him, I immediately stop complaining.

Carly does her usual best to make sure everyone has a positive attitude. While we slurp our chicken noodle soup, she pretends to see celebrities at every turn. She tells us the actor who played the dad on one of our favorite Nickelodeon shows

glimpse

just sat down. Matt, Umberto, and I turn to catch a glimpse, but he's not there. After a few more times, it's a case of the Carly Who Cried Wolf and we ignore her.

Carly shrugs. "Just trying to make the time go by," she says. "We *could* see a movie star."

I smile at her attempt to always make everything fun—even in a disaster. But when we join a group watching the live reports on the TV in the corner of the cafeteria, I realize even Carly's optimism can't fix everything. The reporter on-screen stands in front of a raging fire talking about how many people have been evacuated and how many are without power. There's a gasp from the group when a tree suddenly falls behind him and the reporter has to jump out of the way. Just as we're about to see him scramble to safety, the TV screen goes dark—along with the rest of the gym.

Someone screams and it takes me a moment to realize it's Carly. I blindly reach out to find her and after a few seconds I do.

"I hate that I'm still afraid of the dark," she whispers. "I feel like a two-year-old."

I whisper that it's okay but part of me is almost glad our roles have switched. Carly is always so good at everything, so competent. It's rare when I'm the one that gets to help HER. I tell her the high school prob-ably has a backup generator and we'll have power soon.

After a few minutes of crowd murmuring that gets increasingly

competent

generator

louder, one of the Red Cross women addresses us with an old-fashioned megaphone.

"We're having some technical difficulties with the generator," she says. "Hopefully we'll have it up and running soon. We're going to try to keep things organized, so if you could all slowly make your way to your cots, that would help immensely!"

Carly grabs my arm as we try to find our way back to our corner of the gym. I squint through the crowd to see if Umberto's okay and of course he is; he's one of the most independent kids I know. He's assisting two younger kids who are trying to locate their parents. Not surprisingly, Matt uses the darkened room as an opportunity to swipe some extra granola bars from the food table.

immensely

When we finally reach our cots, I see that Mom's lined up several bowls of water against the wall. She must be able to tell that Carly is a little anxious because she immediately gives her a job refilling the bowls for all the dogs. The guy next to us has two Labrador retrievers that look like they just want to chase squirrels on the lawn instead of being cooped up in a gym.

Join the club.

Mom tells me to keep Poufy away from the other dogs by starting her bedtime ritual. I find the navy-blue tab in the binder with the instructions. Without a bathtub, blow-dryer, or sound system at our disposal, I have no choice but to skip to step five and give Poufy a good brushing. I have no idea what the difference is, but there are separate brushes for her back and belly.

I look around to make sure Oliver or his buddies aren't spying on me before I put away Poufy's tiara and dress her in her nightgown. I hate to admit it, but with her tiny nightcap and teddy bear she's pretty adorable. I snap a picture for her Instagram account and hand her the phone to hit share.

nightcap

Mom approaches and I'm relieved she doesn't pass along another message from Darcy.

"I'm sure we'll be able to drive home tomorrow," she says. "Firefighters and people from the power company will be working all night. Let's pray the winds don't shift and make things worse."

It's not often Mom talks about

praying, so the seriousness of the situation definitely sinks in.

Matt hold up his phone. "If there's no power, that means there's no way to charge our cellphones. I'm only at nineteen percent."

I check my own phone and suddenly panic. "I'm at eight!"

"You may want to power off and save whatever battery you have for tomorrow," Dad says.

I know if I complain, my parents will come down hard, so I keep my mouth shut. But all I'm thinking is *How am I supposed to go to bed on a cot in a gym with tons of people around without playing on my phone to fall asleep?!* I know I should be happy my friends are here—my parents too—but how will I endure this disaster without my phone as

endure

company? Before I power off, I run through my apps to make sure I'm not missing anything. I laugh out loud when I see the meme from Matt. He must've taken a picture of Oliver when he wasn't looking. In the photo, Oliver is probably stretching but it looks like he's scratching his butt. The text below the photo reads *SCRATCH & SNIFF.*

I love having a friend who takes the time to make a joke for an audience of one. I power off my phone and dive underneath the scratchy wool blanket and try to sleep.

MORNING HAS BROKEN

THE NEXT MORNING, I'M SHOCKED when I wake up and it's still dark. According to the analog clock on the wall, it's 5:50. I can't remember the last time I woke up this early. Who knew you could get a good night's sleep on an aluminum cot in a high school gym?

Dad and my friends are still sleeping but Mom's awake sipping coffee from a Styrofoam cup.

analog

aluminum

"The power's back up," Mom whispers.

Before she can utter another word, I grab my phone and race to the charging station.

Mom follows behind me and, after our phones are plugged in, tells me most of the roads are still closed and it'll take a while but we can head home as soon as everyone wakes up. Part of me wants to rouse my friends so this evacuation nightmare can finally end, but another part is enjoying the quiet of the morning. Like Mom savoring her cup of coffee, I let the morning seep in slowly.

seep

Mom motions for me to follow her to the window. I assume it's to show me the effects of the fire, but instead it's to watch the sunrise.

"I'm not sure I've ever seen a sun-rise," I whisper.

"They're pretty great," Mom says. "I see a few a week and never get tired of them."

gentleness

The gentleness of the moment almost makes me want to become a morning person like my mother.

Almost.

As other people begin to rise, I hurry to the food table to grab one—then another—doughnut before they're gone. It takes all the patience I have not to make noise and wake up my friends. I make my way back to the charging station. When my phone battery percentage finally gets to 20 percent, I yank the cord out of the outlet and head back to my cot.

"What the ..."

The first photo I see on the meme site is one of me. It's the same meme Matt forwarded me that Oliver took of me mid-sneeze.

The caption reads:

BOO-HOO. MY DOG FARTED ON ME.

The first hashtag listed under the meme is #PrincessPoufy. My stomach sinks through the floor; that one hashtag was all it took to spread my face through the Internet in a wildfire of its own.

Someone else has taken the picture and reposted it with this:

BOO-HOO. MY DOG PEED ON ME.

Then:

BOO-HOO. MY DOG STOLE MY TIARA.

And:

BOO-HOO. MY DOG BEAT ME IN FORTNITE.

NO NO NO NO NO! I look around the gym and spot Oliver's friend Brian, with the trucker hat. He's got a croissant in one hand and his phone in the other. He wears a giant smirk and looks me straight in the eyes.

croissant

New memes continue to scroll through my phone.

BOO-HOO. POUFY THINKS I'M UGLY.

BOO-HOO. WHICH ONE OF US IS THE PET?

I feel someone standing behind me; it's Matt, barely awake, looking over my shoulder at the memes.

He shakes his head and yawns. "Looks like you've gone viral."

FINALLY LEAVING

I CAN'T GET MY FAMILY AND friends out of the evacuation center fast enough. My parents pack up our stuff and return the linens to the Red Cross while I hurry my friends to the parking lot. The air feels heavy, ashen, and gray like we've landed on another planet.

ashen

Traffic is backed up and the canyon side of the road remains scorched and smoking.

Dad shakes his head. "The hill-side is decimated," he says. "It'll be years before the trees grow back."

decimated

I realize worrying about my meme problem in the middle of this devastation isn't the most mature thing but I can't help asking, *WHY ME?* Even as I ask the question, I acknowledge that it's pretty selfish— but still...

Carly has the same antennae for what people are thinking that my mom does and immediately asks what's up. I show her the meme site, which now has twenty-three memes making fun of me.

Make that twenty-four...

Twenty-five...

She shrugs, hands me back the phone, and tells me it's no big deal.

"That's because it's not YOU who's

getting made fun of," I say. "Every-one in our school is on this site."

She points to the destroyed canyon surrounding us. "They said twenty-five families lost their homes and over six thousand acres were burned. THAT'S a disaster."

Tell me something I don't know.

I sulk for a while till I realize we're going the wrong way. When I ask Dad, he tells me we're stopping by Darcy's house to make sure there's no damage.

"I'm sure you guys want to get home after all this excitement," Mom says, "but it's only fair we give Darcy an update."

"When are we ever going to have full access to a trampoline, pool, and rock-climbing wall again?" Matt asks. "If the house is fine, I say we stay."

I can tell by Mom's face that Matt's suggestion is not an option.

The traffic is bumper to bumper. "Look at all these rubberneckers," Dad says. "Everyone wants to examine the damage."

rubberneckers

Yet when we pass the annihilated hillside, we slow down and gawk too. I guess being nosy and curious comes with being human.

annihilated

"I hope we get to the house soon," Mom says. "The air quality in this car must be terrible."

I don't know if it's the air quality or the stop-and-go traffic we've been stuck in for over an hour, but Poufy starts shaking in her car seat.

"Something's wrong with Poufy," I say.

As soon as the words leave my mouth, Poufy vomits a wet mound of half-digested chicken liver and wild rice.

"PUPPY PUKE!" Umberto yells.

Carly claps her hands over her nose and mouth like she might vomit too.

"WE JUST CLEANED THESE SEATS!" Matt shouts.

"It's okay," Mom says in the calmest voice she can muster. "I've got some wipes in the glove compartment."

I've had to clean up when Bodi's gotten sick before, so I take the situation a little better than my friends.

"You should post THIS on Poufy's Instagram," Umberto jokes.

"NO," Mom commands from the front seat. "We aren't breathing a word of this to Darcy."

We leap out of the car as soon as

Dad puts it in park and are shocked to see the front yard of the Malibu house covered in ashes.

"It looks like Grammy's house at Christmastime." I have a sudden urge to make snow angels the way I do in my grandmother's yard after a New England blizzard.

blizzard

Firefighters are packing up their gear in the driveway. I've seen lots of fire trucks zoom down the street before—honking for cars to pull over—but I don't think I've ever seen actual firefighters at work.

I'm almost too busy watching them coil up the hoses to notice the damage the fire's done to the house.

Looking through the holes burned in the front and sides of the house, I can see the white living room is now black and gray. The chandelier

chandelier

dropped from the ceiling onto some two-by-fours that used to be the sofa. The kitchen cabinets are scorched and the giant sliding glass door is cracked.

conifers

"Even the microwave melted," I say in disbelief. "I didn't know that was possible."

Dad is more captivated by the hillside. "You think any of these trees will grow back?" he asks.

regenerate

"The conifers probably won't regenerate," one of the firefighters answers. "It's too bad because some of these cypress were fifty feet tall." He lets out a low whistle. "Really changes the landscape with them gone."

cypress

It's amazing how a place can go from the Taj Mahal to uninhabitable within a matter of hours.

uninhabitable

Mom takes pictures of the devastation with her cell. "I'm sure Darcy has insurance, but still..." She shakes her head.

"Hey, do you think if we ask the firefighters, they'll let us climb on the truck?" Matt asks.

The kid is my best friend but even I have to admit the timing on his idea is terrible.

"We're NOT asking the firefighters for a ride on the truck OR seeing if they'll turn on the siren," I say. "They've got bigger problems to deal with right now."

"Uhmmm...little help here?"

Umberto's wheelchair is stuck in the mud near the front door. Before Matt and I can get to him, two firefighters lift Umberto out of the sludge and bring him onto the driveway.

sludge

The woman firefighter grabs a hose from the truck and rinses off Umberto's tires.

My parents thank the firefighters for their hard work. Then Mom sits down on the soggy steps to send the pictures to Darcy. Poufy looks at the ruins of her home and whines. She may have been spoiled with her own bedroom and a closet full of clothes, but it doesn't matter how many possessions you have—when you lose everything, you lose everything.

soggy

I sit next to Mom and scoop Poufy into my arms. "It's okay, girl. We'll take care of you. You'll get to meet Bodi."

The drive home is quiet. Even Carly refrains from spreading her usual cheer and stares silently out the window.

Between the traffic and the road closures, it takes us three hours to drive eleven miles. I don't need to ask my friends if they want to hang and watch YouTube at my house. We're so happy to be home, and their parents are all waiting at our house when we arrive.

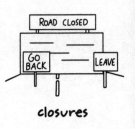

closures

Listening to Matt tell his mom about the evacuation, I try not to laugh. In Matt's version of the story, the fire burned two million acres and we barely escaped with our lives.

Dad puts his hands on Matt's shoulders and assures his mom that Matt is exaggerating. "The fire was bad enough without making it worse," Dad tells Matt. "A lot of families have to rebuild their lives."

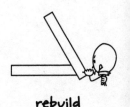

rebuild

Matt nods like he understands but I'm not sure he does.

rubble

charred

Walking through all the rubble changed something inside me. I keep coming back to the image of Darcy's kitchen and the loaf of homemade banana bread Mom left on the counter when we evacuated. Looking through Mom's photos of the house afterward, I couldn't understand why there was a charred brick on the kitchen counter. Did the roof cave in? But when I zoomed in and asked Mom, she told me it wasn't a brick. It was her homemade banana bread, burnt to a crisp.

HOW'S THAT FOR A

REALITY CHECK?

BACK AT SCHOOL

AT SCHOOL, MATT CONTINUES telling his embellished stories about our adventure, but now Umberto chimes in with his crazy take on the events too.

As they describe the evacuation again at lunch, Carly sidles up beside me and whispers, "In the next version, a Pegasus flies in to save the day."

vexing

I'm secretly glad Carly finds Matt's and Umberto's versions of events as vexing as I do. We grab seats at our usual table without waiting for Matt and Umberto.

"I've been so anxious since the evacuation," Carly says. "I made my parents take out the earthquake emergency kit in our garage. It was buried underneath all this old lawn furniture—I insisted we go through the whole kit to make sure we had everything we needed. I even checked all the food expiration dates."

expiration

"Sounds like you're going a little overboard," I respond. "You can't spend every second worrying about bad things that can happen or you'll drive yourself crazy."

overboard

But Carly goes right back to talking about first aid kits and stocking up on bottled water. She finally runs out of steam by the time Matt and Umberto join us.

"I'm guessing you haven't seen this yet." Matt holds up his phone and shows me the latest me-meme.

(Me-meme? Can I trademark that?)

Matt dances the phone in front of my face. "Hello? Earth to Derek!"

The meme of me NOT crying with Poufy on my lap, which everyone in the world—except me—seems to think is hilarious, now has a caption that reads:

BOO-HOO, MY DOG IS SMARTER THAN I AM.

"Sticks and stones," I begin.

"Dude, you're a star," Umberto interrupts. "More kids have seen your memes than watched all your YouTube videos combined."

"These aren't MY memes!" I shout. "They have nothing to do with me."

"Are you sure?" Matt asks. "'Cuz you're kind of acting like a whiny meme right now."

I don't finish the last few bites of my meatloaf sandwich, just grab my tray and leave.

It's one of those rare times I wish the Internet had never been invented.

DISGUSTING!

"DEREK, STOP FIDGETING!" MOM says over the sizzling bacon she's cooking for breakfast. "Between the scratching of my usual mosquito bites and their scab picking, you're giving me the creeps."

sizzling

"Maybe the kitchen table isn't the best place," I answer. "But you've got to admit, picking scabs is more addictive than video games."

I love it when Mom thinks she

mosquito

should be serious and attempts to hide the fact that she's trying not to laugh. She dabs the bacon on a paper towel and puts the strips on the plate in front of me.

As always, the smell of bacon brings Bodi into the room. He's too well trained to beg for food while we're at the table, however that doesn't stop him from sitting by my chair with a non-begging Oh-Is-There-Bacon-Here? expression on his face.

The salty aroma of the bacon seems to have Poufy in a trance. She vigilantly watches Mom in each step of the process with tunnel vision.

vigilantly

"Poufy's mesmerized," I say.

"I'd be shocked if Poufy's ever smelled it before," Mom replies.

Before I can stop her, Poufy

springs onto the table and swipes a strip off my plate. Mom laughs at the stunned expression on my face.

"Let's keep that our little secret." She hands a piece to Bodi to keep things even. "What Darcy doesn't know won't hurt her."

Poufy now stares at Bodi eagerly devouring his bacon, as if she expects him to be a gentleman and offer his prize to her.

It's amazing how different dogs' personalities can be. Poufy may have her good qualities, but no dog in the world could compare to Bodi. I missed him so much while we were in Malibu that I've already taken him on three walks since yesterday.

When I get to school, I instantly feel the dread of my upcoming Lit quiz seep into my body. After bombing the last test, I use the extra time in study period to review my notes. I don't realize I'm picking at my hair until Carly tosses a balled-up piece of paper at me from across the room. I unfold the paper to find one word—*STOP.*

simile

I sit on my hands to keep from scratching and finish reading the section on the difference between a simile and a metaphor.

When it's finally time for the test, I'm relieved to find that I can answer the first two questions easily. As we write our responses to the essay question, Ms. McCoddle walks down each aisle, checking our work.

tunic

Even though she's wearing a tie-dyed tunic and jeans, the way Ms. McCoddle's walking with her hands clasped behind her back makes her seem like a drill sergeant surveying a rookie in boot camp. For once, I don't mind when she stops next to me; I even push my test to the corner of the desk so she can see how many questions I've already answered.

rookie

When I look up, Ms. McCoddle has a quizzical look on her face. But it's not my test that's got her looking so perplexed.

It's my head.

She kneels down next to my chair and whispers, but before she does, she looks on both sides of us to make sure no one's listening.

"Derek, I think you might have lice."

"LICE?"

discreet

Ms. McCoddle closes her eyes, obviously displeased with my outburst. She is trying to be discreet, and now the entire class is groaning at the mention of bugs.

As our teacher tries to quiet the class, I jump out of my seat, shaking my hair like a dog at the beach.

"Gross!" Sophia who is sitting behind me says. "Don't get your cooties on me!"

"There are no such insects as cooties," Ms. McCoddle says. "The actual term is head lice and the singular word is louse."

louse

This might be the worst use of a "teachable moment" I've ever seen but Ms. McCoddle is determined to turn this train wreck of a conversation around.

train wreck

"That's where the word 'lousy' comes from," she continues. "It can refer to something bad, like a lousy slice of pizza, but it can also mean infested with lice."

infested

"I AM NOT INFESTED WITH LICE!" I yell.

It might be psychological, but half the kids in class begin furiously scratching their OWN heads.

"Okay, everybody, back to your tests," Ms. McCoddle says. "Derek, why don't you go see the nurse?"

"Yeah, tell her you feel lousy," Jacob says.

The whole class laughs as I trudge out of the room.

Why is it that whenever I hear people laughing lately, it's always at ME?

CREEPY-CRAWLIES

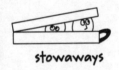

stowaways

carnivorous

MRS. ADOMIAN, THE NURSE, TELLS me there hasn't been an outbreak of lice at our school in three years. I find it hard to believe that a school in a city this size could go so long without insect stowaways but I don't argue.

I'm convinced my lice came from Poufy. Even with all that bathing and grooming, she still managed to pass me her carnivorous critters.

"Lice don't have anything to do with bad hygiene and they don't come from dogs," Mrs. Adomian corrects me. "They feed on human blood and can only survive in the hair on your head. You're just a giant, traveling chicken McNugget to them."

hygiene

If she's trying to make me feel better, she's doing a lousy job. (Yes, I went there. If the entire world can make fun at my expense, I can too.)

When I ask the nurse how to get these freeloading creepy-crawlies off my head, she tells me my parents will have to buy a special shampoo.

"My dad works only twenty minutes away," I say. "He can come get me."

Nurse Adomian takes off her latex gloves and tosses them in the trash. "Having head lice isn't enough of a concern to warrant sending you home. Your parents can pick you up after school as usual."

"WHAT?"

I don't believe it. Not only do I have a village of bloodsucking bugs crawling in my hair, but I have to chauffeur them around for the rest of the school day?!

Sorry, not happening.

"I think I'm going to throw up." (I hate to lie to a medical professional, but this is an emergency.)

"My stomach hurts really bad." I cross my arms over my tummy and rock back and forth to really sell it.

thermometer

Nurse Adomian doesn't say anything. Instead, she raises an eyebrow and sticks a thermometer under my tongue.

"Your temperature is as normal as can be," she says once it beeps.

"It's not like I'm trying to get out of my Lit test," I say. "I already finished it. I just feel too nauseous to go back to class."

"Okay, I'll give your father a call."

It takes Dad a full forty-five minutes to pick me up, so I have to commit to looking woozy longer than I bargained for. It'd be nice if I could lie back and fall asleep, but I can't close my eyes without seeing armies of tiny insects with pincer mouths marching back and forth on my scalp. When Nurse Adomian says my dad is at the front desk, I sprint to the car in record time.

pincer

"I've never had lice before," I rant as soon as I climb in. "This is totally from that evacuation place—the

parasites

blankets were probably full of parasites."

Dad doesn't start driving until I calm down and put on my seat belt. "I thought that too," he finally answers. "We'll pick up some medi-cation and strip the beds and towels as soon as we get home. No big deal."

Except it IS a big deal.

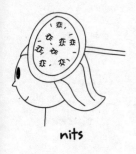

nits

Dad stops at the pharmacy for a nasty solution to get rid of the lice. The comb has the tiniest teeth I've ever seen, supposedly to pull out all the eggs, which are called nits. As if this wasn't bad enough, Mom comes over between patients and wraps a hot towel around my head and makes me sit with it like a turban for half an hour with the shampoo on.

"This is what I get for reading," I tell her.

"Excuse me?"

"I probably got these stupid bugs from one of those toddlers that Carly was entertaining at the evacuation center."

"There's no way to know where they came from," Mom says. "You could've caught them last week at school and the eggs are just hatching now."

The thought of the word *hatching* when it's applied to something on my scalp makes me almost throw up for real.

"It was probably that surfer, Oliver," I say. "His hair was more tangled than seaweed. He could have a nest of seagulls in there and not even know."

I feel a soft thud in my stomach at the thought of Oliver and his

friends. I dig my phone out of my pocket and head to the meme site.

Please no.

But my wish is unanswered. There on the home page—for all the world to see—is the picture of me NOT crying. The caption underneath it reads:

BOO-HOO, I'VE GOT HEAD LICE.

Oliver doesn't go to my school, so he couldn't be the one who posted this today. Which means someone in my class is making fun of me to my digital face. This isn't fair!

It's only nine o'clock when I decide to head to bed and check out of this epic fail of a day, but Mom stops me on the stairs and tells me to post a good-night photo of Poufy.

"If you're healthy enough to make memes and text your friends, you're healthy enough to take care of your Poufy responsibilities," she says.

I can't believe it. Avoiding Poufy duty was the one silver lining that could possibly come from having lice and it just evaporated.

The next day, I beg my parents to let me stay home from school.

"Even with all the treatments, I'm still probably contagious," I tell them.

My mother combs through my hair with the magnifier on her head that she uses to examine animals. She looks like a miner, sifting around for tiny diamonds instead of nits.

magnifier

"If you don't want to go because you're afraid of being teased, that's a different story," Dad says.

"Of course that's why I don't want to go!"

"Well, that's no reason to stay

sifting

home," Mom says. "I thought you were concerned with the safety of your fellow students."

I glare at them both. It's not even seven in the morning and I'm already tired of their "good cop, bad cop" routine.

"I'll give you a ride on my way in," Dad says. He goes to tousle my hair, then thinks twice and pulls back his hand.

"See?" I say. "YOU don't even want to touch me. I'm a freak. No one gets cooties at my age!"

The doctor-part of my mother takes over as she tells me age has nothing to do with where a parasite will strike. All I know is, today's school day is going to have all the fun of a root canal.

I make Dad drop me off a block

before the school so if there are any jeers I won't have to suffer the humiliation of hearing them in front of a parent.

"Hey, Ant-Man!" Chris shouts from the parking lot. "You gonna show off your vermin superpowers today?"

vermin

I knew today's abuse would be relentless, but I haven't even walked into the building yet.

Matt, Umberto, and Carly are waiting at my locker.

"If you're here to make fun of me, get in line."

Matt shakes his head, like nothing could be farther from the truth. "Just keeping you informed, that's all."

informed

Carly half smiles. "So far, you're the only one infected—so that's good."

Would it be terrible to admit I've been praying for just the opposite—that someone ELSE could join me in this parasitic purgatory?

purgatory

"FYI," Umberto adds, "the memes are starting to go super-viral. The lice one's already gotten three million likes."

"THAT'S IMPOSSIBLE!"

But when Umberto holds up his cell, the numbers speak for themselves.

"Too bad there isn't a way to make money off this." Matt turns to Carly. "Can Derek trademark the phrase Cootie Kid?"

"I DO NOT—" I stop myself halfway through my response and downshift to a whisper. "I do not have cooties."

Maria Gonzales taps me on the

shoulder. "Evan and Tyler do," she says. "And there are four other kids in the nurse's office waiting to see her now."

"You really got the ball rolling on this whole head lice thing," Matt says. "I can't remember anything else in school that you've been first in, can you?"

I want to shove him into my locker but use restraint and walk away.

The question is, what spreads faster—lice or memes?

ANOTHER
UNWELCOME GUEST

THE FACT THAT BOTH THE MEMES and the lice can be traced to ME haunts me all week.

ecology

Ms. McCoddle uses the wildfire to talk about ecology, animal habitats, and emergency preparation. Since Carly's been thinking about this stuff 24/7, she chimes in throughout the impromptu lesson.

impromptu

"If we have power on our phones,

we can use them to monitor any kind of disaster," Carly says. "You can get up-to-the-minute news on Twitter or Facebook if you use the right hashtags."

#overit

#pleasecanwemoveon

Maybe Ms. McCoddle has noticed how anxious Carly's been since the evacuation because she DOESN'T move on. She answers Carly's questions and calls on her every time she raises her hand. By the end of class, we've all made checklists of things to have on hand in an emergency.

"Like lice spray," Billy adds as the bell rings.

I don't bother telling him you don't spray lice to get rid of them, but the last thing I want to sound like is an expert lice exterminator.

exterminator

By the time lunch rolls around, we're ready to talk about anything besides wildfires.

Except Carly.

"So much of it depends on the direction of the wind," she says. "That's what made our fire so much worse."

"OUR fire?" I ask. "Like we own it now?"

She ignores me and holds up her phone. "This eighty-seven-year-old woman in Texas saved every letter that'd ever been mailed to her. After the flood, decades of letters were gone like THAT." Carly snaps her fingers in front of my face.

"You're following old ladies from Texas now?" Matt asks.

Carly flips her hair back and tells him disasters can strike pretty much anywhere. "FYI, Qatar is the safest place in the world," Carly continues. "People who live there have less than a one percent risk of getting hurt in a natural disaster."

"No one's moving to Qatar," I say. "Wherever THAT is."

Carly patiently explains that Qatar borders Saudi Arabia on the Persian Gulf—but she's already lost her audience. Umberto, Matt, and I head to our next class, leaving Carly's geography spiel behind us. As we're about to walk into the classroom, Umberto suddenly screeches to a halt.

geography

"Remember that kid who was helping Oliver post those memes?"

"The kid with the fifty layers of T-shirts or the kid with the trucker hat?" Matt asks.

"The kid with the trucker hat." Umberto points down the hallway. "Doesn't that look like him?"

"It can't be." I squint down the hall at the kid talking to Mr. Demetri. "He lives in Malibu, remember?"

Mr. Demetri hears us talking on the way back to his office. "Brian? His family lost everything in the fire. They're staying with friends in this part of town while their home is repaired, so he'll be attending our school for a while."

NO NO NO NO NO NO NO NO!

Matt pats me on the shoulder. "And you probably thought today couldn't get any worse."

This is not good. Not good at all.

BOO-HOO

I SPEND THE NEXT TWENTY-FOUR hours feeling like a canine with a skin condition because Mom continually uses her magnifying-glass visor to examine my head and sweep through my hair with a tiny comb. She even breaks out the soothing voice she only uses for her four-legged patients—which is almost as embarrassing as having your mom play with your hair.

visor

If Oliver could see this, I'd DEFINITELY have to enter the witness protection program.

Finally, she gives my head a clean bill of health. That's the good news.

The bad news is that almost ten percent of the school is now infested with lice. It's obviously not all from me—I don't even KNOW that many kids—but since I was the first one diagnosed, I get all the credit.

diagnosed

Also in the bad news department, I spend most of my time hiding from the new kid, Brian. Matt says he probably won't even recognize me, which might have been true—if it weren't for the memes. There are over 400 now, ranging from hilarious to dumb to random to just plain mean. A few new ones are added every hour. It's too bad this multitude of jokes isn't bringing me money or fame—just aggravation and embarrassment.

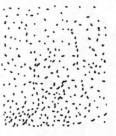

multitude

I evade Brian for four solid days before I literally run into him outside the gym.

He stares at me blankly, which I take as a good sign. I pick up my math book from where it fell on the floor and scurry away with a grin.

aggravation

"Not so fast," Brian calls.

I wheel around slowly and face this kid who's probably got forty pounds on me. Today's hat reads *Jumbo Shrimp*, which is an oxymoron I learned from Carly but could also be a restaurant in the marina.

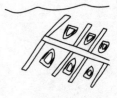

marina

"Haven't I seen you before?" He breaks into a smile.

Before I can tell him we were both

in the evacuation center in Malibu, he answers his own question.

"You're the meme kid with the dog!" He looks around the hall and shouts, "The BOO-HOO kid goes here!" He shrugs. "Who knew?"

"My name is Derek—that's not my dog and I hardly ever cry." *Unless you count the day they came to take away Frank.*

Brian barely listens; he's too busy typing into his phone. "Hold on, this is perfect."

When he finishes, he holds it up for me to see.

It's yet another meme.

This time the caption above my face reads:

BOO-HOO, I DROPPED MY BOOK.

Brian looks at me and smiles. "You can't say it isn't true, right?" He opens the double doors to the gym and whistles under his breath. "This new school is going to be FUN."

I'm guessing he doesn't mean for me.

PRETTY PRINCESS

AS IF GOING TO SCHOOL WITH A bully isn't enough, the entire week-end winds up being all about Poufy. Instead of spending valuable not-in-school time shoving cartoons and cereal in my face or racing Matt down the street on my skateboard, I'm stuck in Mom's office playing beauty parlor.

Having Poufy with us these few

weeks makes me realize just how low-maintenance Bodi is. Poufy's doggy nanny was supposed to take her back by now, but her parents lost their house in the fire, so she's been tied up with them. I can't imagine how she keeps up with all of Darcy's requirements on top of caring for several other dogs. I will never complain again about taking Bodi for walks or picking up his poop.

requirements

grooming

By now, even my mother thinks Poufy's grooming regimen is extreme.

"I don't see why I can't hose her off in the backyard like Bodi," I say.

She reads from the manual. "First we rinse her in mineral water," Mom says. "Then use the aloe shampoo, followed by the shea butter conditioner." She shakes her head. "I wish

telepathic

pageant

conscience

diva

someone would give ME a spa treatment like this."

"How about we pretend we already did all that stuff?" I ask. "It's not like her owner will ever know."

"I wouldn't be so sure," Mom says. "Darcy has a telepathic connection to this dog."

I stand beside Poufy like I'm introducing a contestant in a beauty pageant. "She looks perfect just the way she is."

Mom thinks about it but her conscience gets the better of her and she says we have to go through with the routine. I tell her on one condition—Bodi gets the star treatment too. It will be twice the work, but it's only fair since Bodi has to share the house with a diva dog until Darcy gets back.

When Mom agrees, I run upstairs to find him and bring him over to Mom's clinic.

Bodi's not as excited about the prospect of a fancy bath as I thought he'd be, although once he sees Poufy in the tub, he hops in and wants to play.

I know Poufy's owner says she's not good with other dogs, but you'd never know it by the exuberant yipping the dogs do while we wash them. Even though Bodi is far from dog-show material, Poufy is really enjoying her time with him.

exuberant

Mom's vet offices are tiled, so she doesn't mind when the dogs jump out of the tub. I ask Mom the obvious question as we get ready to trim the dogs. "Don't you have techs who do this for a JOB?"

internship

Mom smiles and tells me she never gets to bathe the animals anymore and sometimes misses it. As she dries off the two dogs, she tells me about an internship she had in vet school where her roommate got a thermometer stuck in a Rottweiler's butt.

"I went straight to ear thermometers after that," Mom says.

I love it when Mom tells stories about her and Dad's life together before I was born. I'm always amazed at the countries they traveled to and the friends they made. Dad actually used to be a national poker champion and I've hardly ever seen him play cards.

I assume we're going to let the dogs air-dry but the instruction manual says we have to blow-dry

Poufy with the setting on low, standing eight to ten inches away. The book also has step-by-step photos with how to style her hair as well as how to tie her ribbons.

"Poufy's owner must have a lot of time on her hands," I tell Mom.

But Mom corrects my assumption and tells me Darcy still runs her multimillion-dollar tech company. I imagine a staff of minions like the doggy nanny working on Poufy's needs during their lunch hour.

assumption

"Please tell me I don't have to Instagram this," I say.

"You Instagram everything else," Mom says.

"Of MY stuff," I complain. "Not on a stupid dog's account."

Mom laughs. "Don't call Poufy

digestion

'stupid'—it'll upset her digestion. That's on page seventy-two."

I can't tell if she's kidding.

I know I don't have to, but I stick around to watch Mom trim Poufy's nails, clean her ears, and brush her teeth. I'm about to remind her to do the same for Bodi but she automatically does.

When she's finally finished, I snap a photo of the squeaky-clean Poufy and Bodi together and hold it out to Poufy so she can send it out to her followers.

Within half an hour, Carly's at the back door cooing about what a cute couple Bodi and Poufy are.

"I can't believe you follow a dog on Instagram," I tease.

"Wrong—I follow several dogs on Instagram."

Before I can let Carly in, a van pulls into the driveway behind her. It's pink with pictures of cartoon dogs all over it. The writing on the side of the van says PUPPY PEDICURES.

pedicures

A woman wearing a white lab coat gets out carrying several small cases. "Darcy just saw the photo of Poufy on Instagram and wanted me to come by for a quick touch-up," she says.

I tell her we just DID Poufy's nails.

"But, honey, you didn't DO them," the woman says.

The woman stands alongside Carly who says, "THIS, I've got to see."

Before the woman gets to explain all this to Mom, Darcy texts to tell my mother Poufy needs to have some designs on her nails—especially after the trauma of the evacuation.

trauma

Their conversation is pretty one-sided and Mom doesn't look too happy when she hangs up.

"Darcy also wants to know if you wouldn't mind cropping Bodi out of the photo you posted," she asks. "She thinks it'll get more likes if it's Poufy alone."

ire

I'm always glad when my mom's ire isn't aimed at me.

By the time I crop the photo and Poufy posts it again, the woman with the lab coat has finished one of Poufy's paws and asks what I think.

Carly is grinning, waiting for my response.

"Are those ladybugs?" I ask. "How'd you paint them so tiny?"

minuscule

The woman holds up a minuscule bottle of nail polish and tells me it's all in the tools.

Carly informs me that she's next in line.

"How about you, Derek?" the woman asks. "Wouldn't you like me to do your nails while I'm here?"

I tell her no thanks and shudder at what THAT meme would look like—not to mention what it would do to my reputation.

If there's anything left of it.

At school on Monday, Carly's so excited about the pink-and-white doughnut design—complete with sprinkles—the woman painted on her nails that she's wearing a neon pink T-shirt with white leggings to match. I'm just glad she's finally focused on something else besides evacuation plans and emergency ration kits.

Matt spent the weekend doing touristy things because his cousins

touristy

were in from out of town, and Umberto's brother graduated from college, so they had a big party. No one else had to put ribbons in a puppy's hair and post it to Instagram.

"My cousin Luke couldn't believe you and I are friends," Matt says. "He thinks you're a celebrity."

"Because of the memes?" I ask. "Who wants to be famous for crying and reading *Goodnight Moon*?"

"Stop complaining," Matt says. "You've got fans in Michigan—that's GREAT."

I'm not sure *fans* is the right word for people who are poking fun at you, but I don't feel like arguing and head to class instead.

When I get there, Brian is standing in front of the science room, blocking my way.

I gather my strength to deliver

the speech I prepared this weekend. "I'm sorry your house burned down," I say. "And I'm glad your family has friends in the neighborhood you can stay with. But that doesn't mean you can come to my school and humiliate me."

Brian looks at me blankly. "I'm sorry, do I know you?"

I roll my eyes. "You seem to know who I am when it comes to creating memes."

He shakes his head. "Sorry, dude, I don't think we've met. I'm Brian." He actually extends his hand, expecting me to shake it.

Is it possible he doesn't remember our conversation last week?! Or the fact that we were stuck together at the evacuation center? I feel stupid leaving his hand hanging there, so I reach over to shake it.

As soon as I do, he yanks it back. "Of COURSE I remember you." He pretends to rub his eyes. "BOO-HOO, my dog lost her tiara."

"IT'S NOT MY DOG!" I shout. "I just rescued her from the fire."

It's a slight exaggeration but also kind of true.

"Derek Fallon, stop yelling," Ms. Meyers scolds as she walks by. "Don't you boys have somewhere to be?"

"I'm new here," Brian tells her. "Brian Ralston—nice to meet you."

retract

This time when he holds out his hand, he doesn't retract it.

"Nice to meet you, Brian, but I need you both to get to class."

Brian spins on his heels and walks toward the media center.

Matt, Billy, and Tommy approach me in the hall.

"That kid is trouble," Matt says.

"Who is he?" Billy asks. "Is he new?"

"He's an underwear model for a chubby kids catalog," I answer.

Billy and Tommy laugh and head to class. Matt holds up his phone. It's a new meme, posted seconds ago. Same photo, new words.

BOO-HOO, MY DOG WON'T SHAKE MY HAND. MUST BE THE LICE.

I've got to get Brian transferred out of here. FAST.

RETALIATION

epidemic

budge

I'M ALMOST LATE FOR SCHOOL because Mom insists on checking my head for lice AGAIN. I tell her fifty times that the lice epidemic is winding down and I've been lice free almost a week but she won't budge.

"It's a good thing I insisted, because you've got a whole new batch," she says.

I jump up from the kitchen table and tell her that's impossible.

"Calm down." Mom swats my arm. "I was just kidding."

"Lice aren't funny," I answer.

"Now there's a catchy meme," Mom says. "Get it? Catchy?"

I head to school, leaving my mother in the kitchen laughing at her own joke.

Matt grabs me at my locker before I have time to hang up my Dodgers cap. "Guess what Teddy and Jian were talking about on the bus?" he asks. "How Brian from Malibu models chubby under-wear!"

If this had been during lunch, milk would've shot out of my nose. "I was kidding when I told Billy that!"

"Well, he must've told Teddy, who told Jian, who probably told Camilla and Jessica." Matt's expression turns serious. "Were you TRYING to start a rumor? Or were you just joking around?"

"OF COURSE I was joking around, I don't fat-shame people!" I say. But since Matt brought it up, an idea begins to germinate in my mind. If I could secretly get a picture of Brian, I could start putting HIM in memes— just like the ones he's made of me.

germinate

Meanwhile, Matt's moved onto the next subject: a volcano that's erupting in Hawaii. But I'm already plotting out where I need to go to snap a picture of Brian.

volcano

I check the time on my phone and try to gauge when I saw him in the science wing the other day. I use my peripheral vision up and down the halls like I'm walking around inside a video game stalking prey.

gauge

My vigilance pays off because

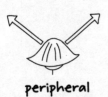

peripheral

just as Brian comes out of Ms. Miller's lab, I'm there. I take the photos in a burst without him seeing and am happy that at least one of them came out.

Brian's wearing a T-shirt with one of those fake tuxedos on the front, so I'll definitely be stealing captions from some DiCaprio memes.

As I walk by Nurse Adomian's office, she gestures for me to come in. I tell her I already got a clean bill of health this morning (which is kind of true) and that I don't want to be late for class (which isn't true at all). She lets me go.

It takes me a while to find Umberto, but I finally do outside his homeroom. I look around to make sure no one can overhear me asking him for a favor.

overhear

"You know Photoshop, right?"

When Umberto nods, I hold up my phone and show him the picture I just took of Brian. "Can you paste a picture of Poufy into this photo?"

"Sure," Umberto answers. "But why?"

I tell him I want to get Brian back for all the memes he's circulated starring Yours Truly. "I want him to know what cyberbullying feels like from the victim's side."

circulated

Umberto frowns. "Dude, that's bad digital citizenship."

citizenship

"He and that guy Oliver started it," I complain. "More than four million people have laughed at me with that stupid Poufy picture. Don't you think it's time for me to turn the tables?"

"No, actually, I don't." Umberto wheels down the hall. "You know that proverb, 'two wrongs don't make a right'? It might be old but it still holds true." He skids to a halt in front of his locker. "I get it—the guy's a jerk but count me out."

proverb

I know what he's talking about— who DOESN'T understand "two wrongs don't make a right"?—but I don't have any other ideas. I slump on the floor beside Umberto's locker.

"Remember when you and I didn't get along? How did we get past all that fighting in the beginning?"

Umberto closes his locker and smiles. "It just took time."

As usual, Umberto's right. I doubt Brian and I will ever become friends but insulting him with memes probably isn't the way to any kind of lasting solution.

Looks like it's back to the draw-ing board.

Again.

SOME ADVICE

I ASK MOM WHEN DARCY WILL BE back from her safari because Poufy's starting to get on my nerves. Not just because we have to wait on her every day like some canine Cleopatra but because looking at her reminds me of Brian and his constant memes. I realize his family has been through a lot, but that doesn't give him an excuse to cyberbully.

Cleopatra

curse

Mom's on her way to surgery but Dad tells me Darcy is held up and won't be back until next week. He hasn't said anything but I think he's had it with Poufy too. He hardly ever swears in front of me, so it was a shock to hear him curse when he tripped over one of Poufy's custom-made squeaky toys. He didn't even apologize when he realized I'd heard him.

While he cuts up chicken for dinner, Dad asks how things are going. I hesitate, wondering how much of the whole meme drama I should share—if at all.

Dad doesn't push; instead he talks about his day and the client who's driving him crazy. "He's asked me to change the art six times already," Dad says. "Everyone says he's an oddball genius but he just seems impossible to please."

"Kind of like Darcy and Poufy?" I ask.

Dad laughs. "I'm never going to thumb my nose at people obsessed with their dogs. I've had dogs my whole life and I've been guilty of spoiling quite a few of them."

I beg Dad to talk about the pets he had growing up, so he wipes his hands on the dish towel tucked into his belt and sits down beside me. I've heard him talk about Zelda the German shepherd and Moxie the Newfoundland before but he's never mentioned Alfie, a greyhound.

Newfoundland

"She was rescued from the track," he said. "We rehabilitated her after she retired from racing. Still the fastest dog I've ever seen."

rehabilitated

I want to find out what happened to Alfie but I'm afraid the story will have a sad ending. Before I can ask, however, Dad volunteers the information. "I came downstairs one morning and she was lying on the kitchen floor, not breathing. I cried like a baby for days."

Dad plays with the edge of the dish towel and I wonder if he's going to cry now.

"How old were you?" I ask.

"Twenty-six," Dad answers. "Kids aren't the only one who get attached to animals."

He swats me with the dish towel and gets back to cooking.

Maybe someone smarter than I am—Umberto, for example—would wonder if Dad had an ulterior motive for telling me this story after asking

ulterior

about my day. Did he happen to be thinking about his old dog or was he paving the way for me to share a bit of myself too?

Whether intentional or not, Dad's plan worked. Before he tosses the cauliflower and chicken into the frying pan, I blurt out the whole meme disaster from A to Z.

intentional

After I finish, Dad nods and waits a moment before answering. Is he going to make me talk to Principal Demetri about this or—God forbid—call Brian's parents?

"It's funny about the Internet," he says. "On the one hand, it's the most important invention since penicillin. On the other hand, it's causing all kinds of problems with privacy, security, and cyberbullying that no one in their wildest dreams could've

penicillin

predicted." He takes the wooden spoon from the canister on the counter and moves the food around the pan. "I mean, who could've imagined people tampering with elections online?"

tampering

We talked about this in class with Ms. McCoddle but hacking into international databases is hardly what's bothering me now.

"I feel bad for kids your age," Dad continues. "As if putting up with regular bullies isn't enough, you have to deal with people hiding behind screen names posting whatever they want with no checks and balances."

"In this case, the bully isn't anonymous," I say. "He goes to my school and brags about his posts."

Dad turns off the gas, then faces me. "Do you want me to get involved?

Or is this something you want to try and handle yourself?"

It's a good question, one I've thought about a lot. A few years ago, I would've begged him to wave a magic wand and fix this situation for me but things are more complicated now. I HAVE to start learning how to take care of life's speed bumps on my own.

"I'll take care of it," I answer.

"Let me know if you need any support." He slides a plate of curried chicken and cauliflower in front of me. "All you have to do is ask."

The dish isn't my favorite, but the food feels warm and comforting going down.

comforting

No! No! No!

I STILL DON'T KNOW WHAT TO DO about Brian but I do feel better after talking to Dad.

Before getting ready for bed, I pose Poufy in one of her pajamas and watch her hit share for one of our last times together.

Poufy snuggles next to Bodi on the end of my bed. I wonder if Bodi will miss Poufy after she leaves. I take a few photos of them to remember her by.

I feel a little ashamed when I swipe by the photo I took of Brian the other day. I can't believe the best plan I came up with was to hurl an equivalent meme back at him. I don't even know what I would've done—maybe something tied to my wisecrack of Brian modeling chubby underwear.

equivalent

I laugh as I type the text above and below Brian's picture. I'm NOT going to spread this across the Internet but I know Matt will still get a kick out of it.

I stare at the meme I've created. Even sending it privately to Matt seems mean and I decide against it.

"Derek—bed!" Mom calls from downstairs.

I toss the phone onto the quilt

and head to the bathroom. When I return, Poufy's laying next to my phone, and the meme I made of Brian is at the top of my feed.

"NO, NO, NO! That wasn't one of your posts!" I yell.

I delete the photo from Instagram then check the meme site as a precaution. After all that's gone on between Brian and me, no one's going to believe I didn't post that meme myself.

I'm shocked when I see the Brian meme, already reposted five times.

I am dead meat.

A STRANGE
COMEUPPANCE

WHEN I TELL MY FRIENDS WHAT
happened at school, Matt laughs so
hard, he snorts.

"That's worse than the dog ate
my homework!" he screams. "No
one's going to believe a DOG posted
that meme!"

"A tiny, prissy dog," Umberto
adds. "Who's not even yours!"

prissy

Carly's the only one not making
matters worse; she's running through

ways to get me out of this. "You should head this off at the pass and go straight to Brian," she says. "Honesty is always the best policy."

"Not true," Matt responds. "Last time I was honest with my brother about his band's new song, he almost choked me in a head-lock."

headlock

Carly rolls her eyes, then scrolls through her phone. "It's already gotten three thousand likes—can't you take it down?"

"You don't think I tried? I read every FAQ to figure out how to remove something after someone reposts it. News flash—you can't!" I pace back and forth in front of the lockers like an inmate waiting to hear about parole.

inmate

Matt is laughing so hard, I'm afraid he might pee his pants.

"Stop it!" I yell. "I feel BAD about this."

As much as Brian has tormented me these past couple weeks, I know what it's like to be on the victim end of the bullying equation. What I didn't realize was how bad it felt being on the BULLYING side. Since last night, my whole body stings as if I stayed too long in the sun. That painful sunburned feeling will hopefully go away. Still, I've been left with a prickly sensation reminding me I did something wrong. Poufy may have been the one who hit share but deep down I know I'M to blame too.

$$\begin{array}{r} 17 \\ +\ 3 \\ \hline 20 \end{array}$$

equation

Matt suddenly stops laughing and points to Brian heading down the hall. He does NOT look happy.

"I've got a test," Umberto says as he races away.

"You're on your own," Matt tells me.

The only one of my friends who appears unafraid is Carly, who stands beside me ready to take the heat.

"This is on me," I tell her. "I'll catch you after class."

Carly reluctantly leaves me face-to-face with Brian.

"I can't believe you lowered yourself to fat-shaming," Brian says. "That's as mean as you can get."

But when I look at the expression on Brian's face, I'm shocked to see he's not angry.

He's hurt.

"Actually I didn't post that meme," I begin. "I did create it but wasn't going to send it—Poufy did it."

"I can't believe you're blaming that stupid dog!'

"I don't expect you to believe

me. I don't expect ANYBODY to believe me. But it wasn't intentional. I changed my mind, I swear."

Brian shakes his head, staring at his phone. "Out of all the things to make fun of me for...I try not to overeat but it's hard. Especially with nachos."

"Who can say no to nachos?" I sit beside him on the floor. "I could eat them 24-7."

"Piled with guacamole." After a moment, Brian turns to face me. "I'm sorry I posted all those memes of you and that dog. I got carried away but it's wasn't cool."

guacamole

It's not the heartfelt apology I'd hoped for but it's certainly a start.

"I'm sorry I made fun of your weight," I say. "Even if I wasn't the one who posted it."

heartfelt

Brian tells me he still doesn't believe me, but when he holds out his hand this time, he doesn't pull away when I shake it.

He reaches into his backpack. "Some friends and I are having a fund-raiser for families who got displaced by the fire. It's at the skateboard park on Venice Beach on Saturday—we got a permit if you and your friends want to skate too."

displaced

He hands me a flyer. "Remember how fast the fire spread through the canyon?"

"Like how fast memes and lice can spread?" I ask.

Brian laughs. "Hopefully some other things can spread too—like these flyers." He offers me a stack of leaflets from his bag. "Are you going to pass these out or make the dog with the tiara do it since she's so good with getting the word out?"

"Very funny."

Out of all the scenarios I imagined last night—most of them ending with me getting the snot beaten out of me—I never would've come up with this one.

I hand out every last flyer on the way home.

TV TIME

POUFY'S OWNER IS FINALLY BACK from her African photo safari, which means I'll be able to return to being a NORMAL dog person, instead of catering to a spoiled canine celebrity who got me into a ton of hot water. I spend most of Saturday morning on Poufy's hygiene so Darcy can't complain. Mom's got several vet techs working right next door but their schedules are full, so I'm the primary person in charge of Poufy today.

primary

I don't just brush her teeth with an old toothbrush the way I do Bodi's; I use a special square of gauze and clean each tooth one by one. I also brush her, take the excess hair out of the metal comb, then brush her AGAIN. I spend more time cleaning Poufy's ears than I've ever spent cleaning mine.

gauze

When I'm finally finished, I go find Bodi, who's patiently waiting on the couch. If he's jealous of all this attention I've been giving to Poufy, he doesn't let it show, just happily wags his tail when he sees me. Watching old Westerns has always been one of our favorite things to do together, so I settle in next to him and turn on the TV.

jealous

dingy

Poufy peeks around the corner to see what we're doing. She's so squeaky clean, everything else in the room looks dingy—including me and Bodi. I just hope all this emphasis on grooming doesn't rub off on me.

When the cowboys on-screen ride to the ranch, Poufy jumps onto her hind legs in front of the TV. She barks at the horses as if they're really standing in the room. Bodi's spent so much time watching animal shows he knows the horses aren't real but Poufy keeps yipping at the screen as if they are.

At first I think she's scared or even threatened, but then I notice her tail wagging, almost like she wants to play.

Her enthusiasm must be contagious because Bodi climbs down

from the couch and stands along-side the TV barking too. I take out my phone and film a short video, making sure to add all of Poufy's hashtags before posting it.

"This time you CAN hit share," I tell her. Poufy dutifully touches the screen with her nose, unaware of all the trouble she's caused. I know Poufy's owner says she doesn't get along well with other animals, but I'm starting to suspect Poufy's just never had the chance to play with other pets. Judging by the way she jumps up next to Bodi and lays her head on his back, I'd say she LIKES interacting with other dogs.

Bodi hasn't had another mammal friend to watch cowboys with since Frank, so I'm glad to see Poufy relax and enjoy his company. Just as the good guy is about to kick butt in the saloon, Mom walks into the den, grabs the remote, and hits the pause button. She's wearing her scrubs and her surgical mask is hanging off her face.

"I've got a full day but I keep getting texts from Darcy." She pulls her reading glasses down off the top of her head and reads from her phone. "'It's too stressful for Poufy to be with other dogs.'"

"Does she mean Bodi?" I yell.

Mom shakes her head. "Darcy is too much." She holds up the picture on Poufy's Instagram stream where Poufy's standing with her face pressed against the television screen, checking out the horses. "'Poufy needs to be at least eighteen inches away from magnetic fields. She also should

magnetic

be on four legs, not two, but of course, being a veterinarian, you already know that.'"

Mom's phone dings with yet another text. "'Please let me know if there are any sections of Poufy's instruction manual that need clari- fication.'"

clarification

Mom looks mad enough to throw her phone across the room—which she'd probably do if phones weren't so expensive to repair. "How did she even have Wi-Fi while on safari?" Mom asks. "Was someone walking behind her with a satellite dish?"

satellite

It thrills me to see Mom irritated with someone who isn't me. She looks exasperated when she tells me to remove the posts. Her face soft- ens, however, when she looks over at the two dogs cuddled on the couch.

brawl

"Never mind," she says. "Poufy's fine. Enough of this nonsense—I'm going back to work."

I hit play on the remote to resume watching the barroom brawl but the cowboy doesn't seem like such a tough guy anymore.

That title now belongs to Mom.

CAT IN A DOG BOWL

BODI

SKATEBOARD
FUND-RAISER

WHEN MATT, UMBERTO, CARLY, AND I get to Venice Beach Saturday afternoon, it's early enough that the boardwalk isn't mobbed. The skateboard park, on the other hand, is already lined with spectators a few people deep.

"Don't pat yourself on the back," Carly tells me. "The flyers you handed out were nothing compared to the social media campaign."

While I was posting and hashtag-ging pictures of Poufy posed next to the TV, Brian and his Malibu buddies were spreading the word about today's fund-raiser in cyberspace.

busker

Brian and his friends who set up the event got busker permits, so two of the older kids are painted silver like battling Tin Men from *The Wizard of Oz*. They're pretending to be oilcan mannequins while different people try to make them blink or smile like the guards at Buckingham Palace. I have to laugh when a young kid shrieks as the Tin Men begin moving like robots.

battling

Performing on the street—even if you have to get a permit and rely on tips people throw into your hat—seems like a pretty fun job. Farther down the boardwalk, there's a woman making a zombie marionette dance to "Thriller" and a guy juggling three bowling pins and—believe it or not—a wheelbarrow. It feels a little weird to be in Venice without my parents, but Umberto's brother, Ms. McCoddle, and a few other teachers are here to help out.

marionette

I still feel bad about making fun of a kid who organized this whole day—not just for his own family, but for all the families affected by the fire. The proceeds from today will only be a drop in the bucket for all that's needed for them to recover, but at least it's a step in the right direction.

proceeds

Watching Brian and Oliver guide young kids on their boards makes me appreciate a different side of them. Instead of goofing around,

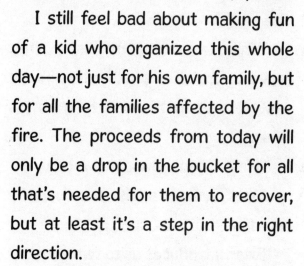

atmosphere

exhibition

they're encouraging and cheering on the little kids. Maybe it's the atmosphere of community but a feeling wells up inside me—a strange happiness connecting me to everyone here. Umberto was right: Being a good citizen—whether online or IRL—is the best way to take part in the world.

While Umberto and his brother leave to watch the exhibition in the bowl, I motion to Matt to grab his board.

"Hey, Brian, how can we help?"

Matt seems a bit surprised by my offer but, as usual, he's game.

Brian introduces us to two younger kids waiting in line for lessons. Matt and I help them put on pads and helmets before we begin.

The afternoon goes by quickly,

with a nonstop flow of people making donations to the cause in exchange for skateboard lessons for their kids.

donations

At the end of the day, Matt motions to the giant skatebowl with its ledges and rails. "Hey, we gotta get some skating in too!"

Brian laughs. "Dude, let's see what you've got."

Maybe it's because the other skaters are exhausted or because the universe is paying us back for volunteering our time, but we get places in the lineup right away and spend the next thirty minutes catching as much air as possible. Carly, Umberto, Eduardo, and Ms. McCoddle lead the cheering section as Matt and I grind our way across the rails.

lineup

When I collapse into bed later

that night, the image that flashes into my mind as I fall asleep is the smile of a little kid today getting to ride a skateboard for the very first time.

GAS PUMP KARAOKE

DARCY?

AFTER SPENDING THE LAST TWO
weeks so focused on Darcy's dog, I
have no idea what she'll be like in
person so I nearly fall over when I
open the front door and find a girl in
an enormous sun hat who looks like
she's still in high school. Because of
how giant her house was—and how
bossy she's been in all her texts—I
was expecting someone a lot older.

enormous

She doesn't greet me, but instead pokes her head in the doorway and calls out, "Poufy!"

The Pomeranian races downstairs and jumps into her arms.

I've seen people kiss their pets before and have certainly watched lots of dogs lick their owner's faces, but I've never witnessed anything like the reunion Darcy and Poufy take part in now. I cough several times to get their attention, which doesn't work. Luckily, Mom comes in and disrupts the lovefest telling Darcy how much we enjoyed having Poufy as a houseguest.

disrupts

Darcy thanks Mom for taking such good care of Poufy, but even as she acknowledges our efforts, I can tell something's bothering her.

houseguest

"I can't imagine what would've

happened if you weren't at the house," Darcy says. "It kills me to think about Poufy going through something as traumatic as an evacuation without you."

"I did have help." Mom stands behind me and places her hands on my shoulders. "Derek was a tremendous assistant."

Darcy smiles. "Ah, yes. You were the one posting pictures of Poufy with that other dog."

My mother and I exchange looks. I quietly go to the kitchen and come back with Bodi.

"Do you mean THIS dog?" Mom asks.

Darcy cowers as if Bodi's poor pedigree might be contagious. She watches in horror as Poufy hops out of her arms to race around the room

cowers

pedigree

with Bodi. The only thing keeping Darcy from blocking the path to Poufy's new friend is the annoyed expression on Mom's face.

"You know, Darcy, in my practice I treat all kinds of animals. And you know what they have in common?"

I figure Mom's going to say they're all in need of medical care but her answer surprises me.

"They're all loved by their owners. No matter how they might appear to other people, all animals are special in their owner's eyes."

I guess not a lot of people talk to Darcy so honestly because she seems unsure of what to say next.

Darcy stares at the two dogs for an awkward moment before finally turning to Mom. "I'm just always so afraid, that's all. I had a Pomeranian as a kid—Fluffy. She never liked to fetch but I kept trying to train her. I threw her a tennis ball and she ended up getting hit by a car."

Mom's face softens and I make a mental note to have an equally sympathetic story ready the next time she's mad at me.

Darcy's story, however, must be authentic because she suddenly bursts into tears. Both Poufy and Bodi hurry to comfort her.

"Man's best friend," I say in a feeble attempt to make Darcy feel better.

feeble

"Woman's too." Mom sits beside Darcy on the couch and gives her a hug. "Unfortunately, dogs get hit by cars all the time," she tells her. "You shouldn't blame yourself for something that happened when you were a kid."

custody

I have to agree with her; it's taken me a while to forgive myself for losing custody of Frank. I know how much carrying around blame and guilt can hurt, so I try changing the subject.

"Can you believe how bad your house got burned?" I ask.

My mother closes her eyes at what I now realize might not be the emotional pick-me-up I was hoping for.

"I came here right from the airport so I haven't been home yet," Darcy answers. "But I'll make you a deal—after it's fixed up, you and your friends can come back and hang out for a day to make up for getting evacuated."

"Can I bring Bodi this time?" I ask.

My mother gives me a look that

tells me that my question is inap-
propriate but I can also tell she's
curious about the answer too.

"Absolutely," Darcy says.

I know it'll be a while before
Darcy's house will be ready, but I text
my friends anyway.

Malibu, take two!

GAMING
TOURNAMENT

I GUESS ONE GOOD THING ABOUT being super-rich is that you don't have to wait for the insurance company to fix your house; you just hire someone to start repairs the next day.

When we pull up to Darcy's house six weeks later, my friends and I are awestruck because it looks exactly the same as it did before, right down to the very last succulent.

succulent

"I can't imagine how much money she spent to get this done so fast," Mom whispers under her breath.

"More than we both made last year," Dad answers.

Darcy shakes hands with Umberto, Matt, and Carly when I introduce them. No one takes it personally when Darcy pulls out sanitizer from her pocket and sterilizes her hands afterward.

sanitizer

"What should we do first?" I ask. "Swim? Climb? Game?"

"Battle Royale here we come!" Matt answers.

commentary

Walking through the house, Darcy keeps a running commentary of everything she does, like a football announcer doing a play-by-play. "First let's get our guests some snacks, right, Poufy? Then play some games?"

The only other person I know who talks to herself all the time is my Grammy; I thought it had something to do with being old and for-

forgetful

getful but apparently other people do it too.

I should have guessed that a girl who started an app company at sixteen and is obsessed with her dog's social media presence would be okay to hang out with—and Darcy is. She watches me and my friends go from one video game to the next with Poufy and Bodi nestled in the

nestled

Pomeranian's armchair. Maybe if we're lucky, Darcy will let us housesit again when there ISN'T a wildfire—or earthquake or flood or mudslide—and we can pretend we're billionaires too.

I ignore the dings on my phone until the end of the battle, then sneak my phone out of my pocket to check it. I'm glad my stomach no longer sinks at the prospect of a new meme making fun of me.

The text is a photo of me on my skateboard at the Venice fundraiser. I'm midway between the wall and the lip of the bowl with a huge grin on my face. It's hands down the best photo ever taken of me on my deck.

midway

The caption reads:

WHEN THEY SAY STOP AND YOU SAY GO!

I doubt this meme will go viral, but I set it as the wallpaper on my phone anyway. Some things are meant to just make YOU happy and don't need to be shared with the rest of the world. I want everything that starts with me from now on to be positive. Maybe hanging out with Carly has rubbed off after all.

By the way, Brian's text reads, *I still don't believe a dog can post memes.*

I laugh and text him back, thanking him for the photo, then go back to hanging out with my friends.

Just another day in paradise.

Have you read all the books in the My Life series?

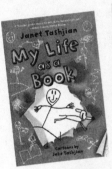

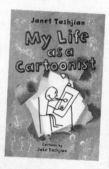

Turn the page to find out!

My Life as a Book

Derek Fallon has trouble sitting
still and reading. But creating cartoons
of his vocabulary words comes easy.
If only life were as simple!

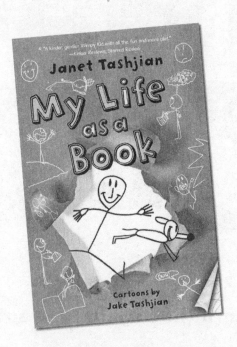

My Life as a Stuntboy

Derek gets the opportunity of a lifetime—
to be a stuntboy in a major movie—
but he soon learns that it's not as
glamorous as he thought it would be.

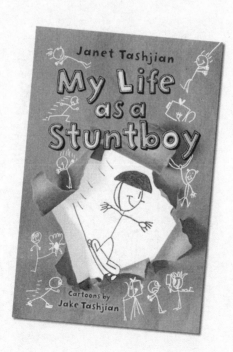

My Life as a Cartoonist

There's a new kid at school who
loves drawing cartoons as much
as Derek does. What could be better?

My Life as a Joke

Now in middle school, Derek just wants to feel grown-up—but his own life gets in the way, and he feels more like a baby than ever.

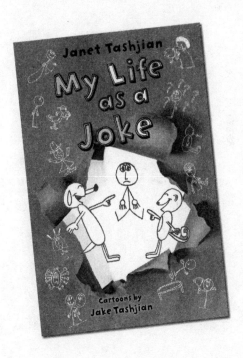

My Life as a Gamer

Derek thinks he's found his calling when he's hired to test software for a new video game. But this dream job isn't all it's cracked up to be!

My Life as a Ninja

Derek and his friends are eager to learn more about ninja culture. When someone starts vandalizing their school, these ninjas-in-training set out to crack the case!

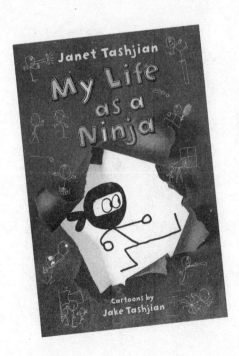

My Life as a Youtuber

Derek becomes a popular YouTuber just as his foster capuchin, Frank, must go off to monkey college, so Derek furiously scrambles to find a reason for Frank to stay. What if Frank became a part of his YouTube videos?

About the Author

Janet Tashjian is the author of many best-selling and award-winning books, including the My Life series, the Einstein the Class Hamster series, the Marty Frye, Private Eye series, and the Sticker Girl series. Other books include *The Gospel According to Larry*, *Vote for Larry*, and *Larry and the Meaning of Life* as well as *Fault Line*, *For What It's Worth*, *Multiple Choice*, and *Tru Confessions*. She lives in Los Angeles.
janettashjian.com
mylifeasabook.com

author

About the Illustrator

Jake Tashjian is the illustrator of the My Life series and the Einstein the Class Hamster series. He has been drawing pictures of his vocabulary words on index cards since he was a kid and now has a stack taller than a house. When he's not drawing, he loves to surf, read comic books, and watch movies.

Illustrator